LILA FOX

EVERNIGHT PUBLISHING ®

www.evernightpublishing.com

Copyright© 2025

Lila Fox

ISBN: 978-0-3695-1181-2

Cover Artist: Jay Aheer

Editor: Lisa Petrocelli

LILA FOX

Lila Fox

Copyright © 2025

Chapter One

Tessa walked into the town bar with her friend, Michelle. She couldn't help when her gaze automatically went to the end of the bar where Dominik, the man of her dreams, always sat.

She froze when she saw he was staring at her. She always caught him looking at her whenever she turned to him and smiled, but he never took a step toward her. She'd lived in the town of Parkersburg for five months and had probably seen Dominik a few dozen times, but it hadn't gone farther than that.

She was tired of waiting for him to make a move and decided that that night, she was going to pull up her big girl panties and go to him. That's if she didn't pee her panties first.

It wasn't that she was afraid of him. He caused shivers to race up her spine, but she knew it had to do with pure hormonal need and never fear. Oh, she knew some, or actually a lot, of people were terrified of him.

But never did he make her feel it.

Everything about the man was large, powerful, and dominant. Even though she never said a word to him, she could tell from across the bar. He had to be close to six and a half feet tall, and she guessed over two hundred pounds. But he was also dark—dark skin from working outside, dark hair, and eyes. The scars from an accident he'd had years before were noticeable, but it didn't lessen her attraction to him.

Someone handed her a drink, and she sipped it while she listened to her friends from work. She tried to be attentive to the conversation, but her attention always strayed to Dominik.

Several hours later, she finally decided to make a move.

"Hey, Michelle, can you hold this for me, please?" Tessa asked.

Michelle reached for the glass and focused on what she was looking at. "Girl, are you really going to talk to him?"

Tessa nodded. "I'm sick of waiting."

"I'm not sure you'll be able to deal with him," Michelle said.

Tessa glanced at her and frowned. "Why?"

"First off, he's huge, and you're tiny. You're also as sweet as can be, and Dominik is the opposite. I've known him for ten years, and he's always been hard to be around, but after his accident..." Michelle shrugged. "He's ten times more difficult. A lot of people are afraid of him, and the damage that was done to his face makes the fear worse. Maybe it would help if he did more than growl and scowl at people."

Tessa scowled. "Are you talking about the scar on his face bothering people?"

"Well, it's hard to ignore. Don't get me wrong.

He's still a hot guy but rougher looking."

"I noticed it, of course, but I really don't see it." Although she hadn't gotten really close to him, it was hard not to see a scar on the side of his face. She knew when and if she got closer, it might look worse, but it didn't matter to her at all.

"I know. I'll never forget the first time we came here, and you saw him." Michelle chuckled. "God, your face was flushed from the attraction, and it looked like you might burst into flames or have an orgasm standing there."

Tessa felt her face grow hot from the blush. Her friend was right. Just looking at him was enough to make the gate to her desire burst open, and she was as close to orgasm as she'd ever been. The fact that they weren't even touching surprised her but also told her they already had a connection.

"I'm going to talk to him."

Michelle grabbed her arm. "Are you sure about this? I don't want you getting hurt."

Tessa patted Michelle's hand. "Yes. I don't want to wait any longer."

"Don't say I didn't warn you," Michelle said.

Tessa smoothed her shirt before turning toward him. With every step she took closer to him, her heartbeat raced faster. She was glad he had his back turned as he listened to the guy next to him. It gave her a few seconds to calm down.

Her arm was taken abruptly, making her stop in her tracks.

"Hey, Beautiful, how about a dance?"

Tessa barely glanced at the man and yanked her arm away from his grip. "No, I'm sorry. I'm on my way to talk to a friend."

The man was forgotten when she was two feet

from Dominik. "Hi."

Dominik turned to her, and his eyebrows shot up. "Hi."

"My name is Tessa. What's yours?" she asked, even though she already knew. She just wanted to keep him talking. The tone of his voice made her nipples harden into tight little stones, and she could feel her cum saturate her panties.

"Dominik."

"It's nice to meet you," she said.

He scowled. She could see why many people were afraid of him. With his eyes narrowed and his jaw clenched, she could tell he wasn't happy.

"Lady, what the hell are you doing?" he asked.

She looked confused. "What do you mean?"

"Standing here talking to me," he said.

Tessa blinked in confusion. "I ... I wanted to meet you."

"Why?"

"Because..." A thought popped into her head. "Do you have a girlfriend?"

"Fuck, no."

"Are you gay?" she asked and fought not to smile. "No."

"Then what's the problem with wanting to meet you?' she asked.

"Because you belong on the other side of the room with the preppy guys."

She frowned. "What do you mean by that?"

"Don't waste your time with me."

"Why?"

"Because we come from two different worlds," he said. "Add to that the fact you're small enough to put in my pocket."

She would have laughed at that if she wasn't so

confused. "Why do you think we're so different besides our sizes?"

"Jesus, woman. You look like a fucking angel, and I look like a monster."

Her teeth snapped together. She hated the thought that he saw himself that way. "That's bull … poo."

He smirked. "It's bullshit, Baby."

The endearment made her want to smile. "All right. It's bullshit."

His scowl darkened. "You're right. I don't like you cursing."

Her smile widened, and she took a small step forward to stand between his widespread legs, surprising him. "Okay."

If anything, he looked angrier. "Don't do that. I can't tell you what to do."

"What if I want you to have the right?" she asked.

She watched as several emotions skittered across his face before it went blank.

"Look, I think you're cute and all, but…"

She felt her stomach tighten in dread. She wanted him to think she was pretty and maybe hot. "You think I'm cute?"

He shrugged. "Yeah."

She took a step back. She wanted to yell at him because she knew he was pushing her away, but he didn't want to. She wasn't going to beg him to like her or take a chance with her. "I see. Well, I'm sorry I bothered you."

She turned without another word and walked away. With each step, she prayed he'd call her back, but it didn't happen.

Michelle took one look at her face. "I'm sorry, hun."

Tessa shook her head. "No. Don't be. You warned me."

"Yeah, but I was hoping it would work out for you."

"Hey, look. I'm going to head home."

"How about I drive you?" Michelle said.

Tessa shook her head. "No. It's only a few blocks away, and I need the fresh air."

Michelle hugged her. "Call me if you want to talk."

Tessa squeezed her friend. "I will. Thank you." She waved at a few more of her friends and walked out the door. She didn't know if she'd be able to go back to the bar because seeing Dominik every time and knowing he didn't find her attractive hurt too much.

Life had kicked her down so many times, but she'd always been able to get up and move on—she would do it this time, too.

When an arm reached out for her, grabbing her in a tight, violent grip as she passed the alleyway, it took her a second to understand what was happening. Then her back hit the brick wall, forcing the air out of her lungs at the impact.

"You fucking cunt, all you had to do was dance with me."

The man started to tear at her clothing. She heard her shirt rip and started to fight.

He slammed her against the brick. "If you don't fight me, I won't kill you."

That just made her fight harder.

He started hitting her with his fist and cursing at the same time, trying to get her jeans down.

One second, she was fighting for her life, and the next, there was nothing. She heard something off to the side and thought this was her chance to run, but she couldn't get her legs to move and slid down until her ass hit the concrete. Her head throbbed so much she drew up her legs and rested her forehead on her knees.

She just needed a minute so she could get enough energy to move.

LILA FOX

Chapter Two

Dominik turned when he heard the bar door open. Something relaxed inside him when he caught sight of the woman he was becoming obsessed with—the one he called his angel.

She was everything he'd ever wanted in a woman, but their worlds were too far apart. He had listened to her for hours as she talked with her friends. Even with her several feet away, he was so in tune with her that he heard her clearly. Every other sound in the place faded.

His gut would twist into a painful knot of need, and his cock would harden until it felt like it would explode. He told himself so many times to ignore her and move on. There wasn't a chance in hell she'd ever want to be with him.

Besides being twice her size, she was everything light and sweet, and he was dark, dominant, antisocial, and cynical. She would never be able to understand his world or him or be strong enough to handle him, both in and out of bed.

He caught the way she looked at him, and it didn't change the fact that they were too different. He also knew that if he did give them a chance and she left him, it would forever damage him. He'd never want to have a relationship with anyone else, so he'd die alone.

Fuck, he knew he was being delusional if he thought he'd want anyone else. Without talking to her, she had ruined him for any other woman.

"Yo, Boss."

Dominik turned to Rey, one of his employees. "What?"

"If you're not going to make a move on that sweet thing over there, I'd like a chance," Rey said.

Fury, unlike he'd felt before, twisted his guts. "Don't even think about it, fucker. Do you understand?"

"But, man, it doesn't look like you're going to do anything besides stare at her. Give the rest of us a chance."

Dominik leaned in closer and lowered his voice. "Let me put it this way. If anyone tries to get together with her, I'll bury you in the concrete foundation of one of our buildings. Tell everyone that."

Rey held up his hands. "Jesus. Yeah. I get it. I'll put the word out."

"Hi."

Dominik turned abruptly to face the person talking—the woman of his dreams. It took a moment to realize she was in front of him and talking to him. "Hi."

He couldn't believe when she stepped closer to him, almost in between his legs. He wanted to snatch her up when she became submissive. Fuck. She was even more beautiful up close. The blue/green color of her eyes was bright, and her smile was friendly.

He tried to determine if his appearance repulsed her, though he couldn't see anything but interest and warmth.

Dominik fought the urge to pick her up and carry her out of the bar. When he raised his arm to pull her closer, he panicked. What the fuck was he doing? He'd already decided it wouldn't be smart to give her a chance. She gave him the out he needed, and he called her cute.

He could tell right away as the light faded from her eyes that he'd done what he intended. He had to grit his teeth when she walked away from him. The fact that her posture and animation had changed told him how much he'd hurt her, and he could have kicked himself.

He watched Tessa say goodbye to her friends and walk out the door without glancing at him. Jesus, the pain he felt was surprising, and it enforced his decision to stay away from her. If it hurt that bad after one short conversation, he'd never recover if they tried and he failed.

Dominik caught sight of one of the guys that had stared at her all night. He had thought he was harmless but then caught the look in the man's eyes before he snuck out the side door. Every male instinct pushed him to make sure she was okay and got home okay. He could do that and stay hidden, so she didn't see him. He threw some bills down and walked out. He'd only gotten a half block from the bar when he heard a scuffle and a woman crying out.

He raced around the corner to see the fucker had Tessa up against the building, trying to pull her pants down and cursing her. She fought, but she was so tiny she didn't have a chance against the guy. By the time he got to them, the bastard had hit her on the head with his fist.

Dominik yanked him away from her and slammed him against the side of the building, several feet away from Tessa. The guy fought the hold he had on his throat. He could tell he was strangling the guy when he started to turn blue, but he didn't care. When he heard Tessa crying and saw her trying to move, holding her clothing in place, he tossed the guy away from him.

"I will find you, fucker, and then you'll pay for touching her."

He walked over to Tessa, hearing the man running the opposite way. He didn't care. His whole focus was on her.

She stood on shaky legs and tried to walk out of the alley. He got to her and caught her when she stumbled. She cried out when he lifted her. He hated the fact that he was frightening her, but he could tell she wouldn't make it another foot on her own.

"Easy, Sweetheart. It's just me. Let me take care of you."

Dominik watched her turn her head and look up at him. When she recognized him, she immediately curled her arms around his neck and pressed her face there. The fact that her trust in him was immediate wasn't lost on him.

He made it to her house. "Where's your key, Sweetheart?"

"I … it's in my jeans pocket," she whispered.

He set her on her feet and waited while she fought to get her key out. He held his hand open, and she dropped it in it. He opened the door, picked her up again, and walked in, slamming it shut with his boot.

He carried her to the sofa, sat her down, and then knelt next to her on the floor. Fuck, with the overhead light, he was able to see her clearly, and he wanted to howl.

"I think we need to go to the hospital, Sweetheart."

Tessa wrapped her arms around her waist and shook her head. "No. Just give me a minute, and I'll be fine."

"How about we clean you up, and I'll check out the damage? If I feel it's bad enough, I'll take you, and I won't care if you argue."

She opened her mouth before it snapped shut, and then she nodded. "Okay."

"Where's the bathroom?" he asked.

She pointed at an open door. "Through my bedroom."

He carefully lifted her again and walked into her bathroom. Everything about it was feminine and smelled like her. He set her on her feet and held onto her arm until she was steady.

Tessa grabbed onto his hands when they started to pull the shredded shirt off her.

"I can get it, Dominik."

He studied her. "Are you sure?"

She nodded.

"Okay, I'll wait in the bedroom. Call out if you need me."

She nodded again.

Dominik closed the door behind him, and it took a lot for him not to go back in and help her. He told himself she'd been through enough already, he didn't want to compound it.

He leaned his shoulder against the doorjamb and listened to her, hoping she didn't hurt herself.

He heard the shower turn on and exhaled. He wiped his hand down his face. Fuck. There were so many emotions going through him. His fondness for her rose along with his desire. When he first got a glimpse of her, he was able to see most of one breast because the bastard had ripped her shirt. Next came the fury that someone had attacked his angel. The guilt built in him when he realized if he had kept her with him, this would never have happened to her.

Jesus, he was so confused. He wanted her with every cell in his body, but his fear of being hurt was stronger. Fuck, what a pussy. If anyone knew what was going through his mind, they would razz him. He knew without a doubt that if he had her and lost her, he'd never be the same.

LILA FOX

Chapter Three

Tessa stood under the water and washed her hair and body twice. She wanted to erase the man's touch. She glanced down at herself and caught sight of the bruises forming and the small cuts she had received from the monster.

She hadn't realized she was crying and pressed a hand to her mouth to prevent a sob from bursting out. She didn't want Dominik to see her like this.

Tessa kept telling herself she'd been through so much in the past and had come out stronger. She knew she'd do the same with her situation, but it would take time.

After she got some control of herself, she squeezed as much water as she could from her hair before twisting it in a towel, grabbing another one, and wrapping it around her torso.

She stood in front of the mirror but didn't look at herself as she smoothed lotion all over her body. She pulled on her robe before pulling the towel from her head. A piercing pain came on the back of her head when she touched it. She raised her hand and felt around, then found a small knot forming. Tessa pushed the thought of how it happened from her brain for the moment. She needed to concentrate on drying her hair. There was plenty of time later to deal with the trauma.

She was careful as she brushed and blow-dried her hair. When it was just wet, she put the dryer away. Her limbs were starting to shake, and she knew from experience that she was crashing from the adrenaline.

When she opened the door, she gasped to find Dominik very close. He moved back a bit and gently grabbed her arm.

"Let's get you checked out."

She shook her head and then cringed as a ragged edge of pain shot down her neck. "I'm fine. I'm a nurse, you know."

"I know that, but you also know what happens to a patient who isn't watched after being hurt. I can tell you're barely holding it together."

"I don't want you to worry…"

He snorted. "Right. Listen," he said and pulled her over to her bed. He sat and pulled her between his legs. "I'm going to give you three choices. Either we go to the hospital, or I call your friends to come here, or I check you over and take care of you. What is your choice?"

She thought about it for a moment. "You."

He nodded. "Where does it hurt?"

"My head."

He raised his hands and felt around. She hissed when he touched the bump.

"We'll need to get ice on this. Let's get the rest done first."

She held still as he pushed the arm of the robe up to inspect her and then went onto the other one. Her hands clutched at the front of her robe when he went to untie it.

"No."

Dominik sighed. "I'm sorry, Sweetheart. I need to check all of you."

"B-but I don't want you to see me like this. I wanted you to want to see me naked."

She could feel herself blushing when he stared at her.

"Let's deal with that later. Your well-being is what's important right now," he said.

He tugged a few times before her shoulders

relaxed, and she let go of the fabric. She closed her eyes as he pulled one side of the robe open and felt around before doing the other side.

"You've got some bruising and a few cuts, but none of them are bleeding right now. I'm mostly worried about your head. What if you have a concussion?"

Tessa shook her head and immediately regretted it. "I don't. I have a small headache but no nausea, dizziness, or trouble focusing."

He looked doubtful but let it go. "Let's get some ice on your head." He held onto her arm, stood, and pulled the comforter back. "Get in bed, and I'll go get the ice."

"Okay."

He helped her get comfortable. "I'll be right back."

She had a strong urge to call him back but stopped herself. He'd already done so much for her, and she didn't want to add to it.

He came back a moment later and gently set the bag of peas on her head. "Tell me if that hurts."

"It feels good."

"I'm going to find you aspirin and get a glass of water."

"The aspirin is in the cupboard to the right of the kitchen sink."

"All right. I'll be back."

She watched him walk out again and concentrated on keeping the peas on her head.

He handed her the pills and water and took the peas from her hand. "Take these. You're going to be sore tomorrow, and this will help."

"I know," she said, swallowing them and drinking all the water. She looked up at him when he stood still beside the bed.

"How do you know that?" he asked.

She could hear the stress in his tone. "I … I've gotten hurt a few times."

He scowled. "When?"

"A long time ago."

She could tell he wanted to ask more questions but was thankful he let it go.

"Do you want to put this back on your head?" he asked.

She shook hers. "No. it's numb right now."

He set the bag on the nightstand and stood staring at her. She saw the emotions racing over his face but only caught the one telling her he was very uncomfortable.

Tessa cleared her throat. "Hey, why don't you head home?"

He scowled at her. "You want me to leave?"

She opened and shut her mouth. "It's not that. You've already done so much for me already. I can't impose anymore."

"You're not. I'm going to lock up, and then I'll crash on the sofa."

"Y-you could lay in here with me," she said but regretted it when it made him even more uncomfortable.

"I'll take the sofa and leave the door open so I can hear you if you need me," he said.

"Okay."

He helped her lay down and get comfortable. "Call out for me."

"I will."

She watched him go and felt tears fill her eyes. The night had sucked so much, but what made her miserable was the fact that he couldn't stand to be near her. What did she expect? He'd already told her he didn't find her attractive and pretty much pushed her away.

Tessa had to stop chasing him. It only

embarrassed him and made her sad. She needed to move on. She was thankful for so much in her life. She'd fought for everything: her job, her house, and her friends, but it just made it all sweeter. There were so many times in her childhood she thought she'd never amount to anything. It didn't help when other people in her life, like teachers or foster parents, would tell her that.

She hadn't had friends because she was sickly as a child, and then moved around too much from foster home to foster home to keep one. She'd learned early to stay as invisible as possible, and if she wanted to make a life for herself, it was on her to do it. She'd read anything she could get her hands on and found medical magazines interesting enough she learned the different words and abbreviations for some of the things. She also studied as hard as she could and was so excited when she received a full scholarship at a college that specialized in medical training.

Tessa had to get a job for extras like clothing or shampoo and things like that. Her scholarship gave her a four-year degree, housing, and three meals a day. She'd taken advantage of the fact that she could take as many classes as she wanted. She got her four-year degree in two-and-a-half years and spent the rest of the time in specialized training for pediatric nurse.

She received job offers before she even graduated but instead moved to where her only friend lived and worked at the same hospital. She'd met Michelle in her last year and had helped her with a few of her classes.

The more they talked and the more time they spent together, Tessa had let down her walls for the first time in her life and let her in. She'd never regretted the fact she'd taken a chance.

All night, she tried to fall asleep, but every time she did, images of what happened in the alleyway haunted her. She wanted to call out to Dominik but knew it would just make him uncomfortable.

The sun was just rising when she finally fell asleep. When she woke up, it was to find Dominik gone, and there was a note saying the police would be there at a certain time. He'd also set up the town locksmith to come and change the locks on the doors and windows. He said nothing about seeing her later.

She let the tears come. She had to tell herself she couldn't grieve a relationship when there had never been one.

Tessa got through the rest of the day. She made a statement about the attack to a few detectives who came to her house. Fortunately, she knew them both.

The woman detective took pictures of her body, noting every mark the man had put on her. It mortified her, but she knew it was going to happen. The locksmith came by while they were there, for which she was thankful. She would have been uncomfortable being alone with a man she didn't know. When she tried to pay him, he told her Dominik had already paid for it.

"I'd still like the bill," she said. "I want to pay him back."

He handed her the receipt before leaving. Tessa said goodbye to the detectives. After she heard their car drive away, she locked the door and moved around the house, making sure everything else was locked up tight.

The rest of the day, she tried to keep herself busy. She made herself lay down and nap, knowing she probably wouldn't be able to sleep that night.

One of the things she got done was to write a check to Dominik with a note thanking him for everything. As much as she wanted to beg him to see her, she cared enough about him to let him live in peace. She put both in an envelope, sealed it, and stamped it. Then, on her way to work the next day, she'd mail it.

The next day was pure hell. Not only was she sore, but she also hadn't gotten enough sleep or eaten, and everyone kept asking her questions about her lack of sleep. She had told a few close friends about the attack, but she didn't want anyone else to know yet. Maybe never.

LILA FOX

Chapter Four

Dominik ripped open another envelope from the stack of letters on his desk. It took him a moment to understand, and then he got pissed.

He didn't want her to pay for the locks, so he ripped up the check before he read her note. If anything, it made him madder. The way it was worded, she wouldn't see him again and wished him well.

"What the fuck?" He reread it a few more times and got the same impression. Even though he knew she was doing it for him, it still hurt. Jesus, was he ever going to find a way to deal with her, or would he have to move away?

That wouldn't be easy since his business and his house were there. He had over thirty employees, so he couldn't just close the business. They'd all lose their jobs.

He carefully folded the note and stuck it in his side drawer. He had no idea why he was saving it, but he couldn't get himself to throw it away.

The next few weeks passed, and every day away from her was getting harder. He fought himself daily, thinking if he went to her, he'd never let her go, and that was what scared him. He couldn't see Tessa putting up with his dominance for long, and then he'd lose her.

The weekend came and another week without seeing her. It had been five excruciating weeks, and if he could just see her across the room, he'd be fine.

Dominik sat at his bar seat like he did every Friday and Saturday, hoping for a glimpse of Tessa. He was just taking a drink of his beer when he heard the door open. He automatically turned to see who it was and about choked on the liquid in his mouth.

She was finally there. His frustration grew when

he saw the noticeable changes in her. There was no animation, and she looked pale. She was also thinner and had dark circles under her eyes, telling him she wasn't sleeping.

Tessa glanced his way and smiled slightly before turning toward one of her friends. He went to stand and go to her but caught himself. For the hundredth time, he reminded himself that she wouldn't be happy with him. They were from two different worlds. She was angelic and had a great childhood. If she knew where he'd come from, she'd run. He made so many excuses, hoping they would help keep him from going to her.

"Hi."

It was like déjà vu. He turned toward his angel.

"Hi," he tried to sound casual.

"I … I just wondered why you didn't call me back when I left a message," she said.

"Why would I?" Fuck, he hated the pain that flashed in her eyes.

"You're right. I just wanted to thank you again for saving me."

He scowled. "You don't have to thank me again."

"I think it will help me get back to normal. I'm close, but that was one thing I thought would help."

"It doesn't look like you're even close to normal. Are you getting counseling?"

"What do you mean? I'm doing fine," she said.

His face darkened. "Hell, you are. You've lost too much weight, and it doesn't look like you've had a decent night's sleep recently."

"I'm trying the best I can."

"You need help," he told her.

She shook her head. "I'm fine."

She held up a hand when he opened his mouth. "This is not your problem." Tessa shrugged. "I guess I just had to say it one more time. It's been a while since I've seen you, and you probably already forgot about it…"

"That's not something I'll ever forget," he told her.

She looked away. "Is there any chance we can go somewhere and talk?"

"For what purpose?" The longer she stood next to him, the harder it was getting to push her away. "Listen, any relationship between us would never work. You and I are from two different worlds."

Her brows snapped together. "What does that mean?"

"I'm from the wrong side of the tracks. I grew up with a mother who was a drunk and only cared about me because she got extra money for me every month."

Her face paled. "So that's the reason you think we're different?"

He nodded. "That's the main one. There are others."

"What are they?" she asked.

God, he was about ready to lose it. He spotted one of the female bartenders who always had a thing for him, but he'd never been interested. "Hey, Monica." He waved over Tessa's shoulder.

Monica walked over to him and wrapped an arm around his neck before kissing him on his cheek. Jesus, the pain that filled Tessa's eyes made him furious at himself.

"I'll leave you to your date," Tessa said. "But you shouldn't assume anything about a person because you'll most likely be wrong."

"What does that mean?" he asked.

She shook her head sadly. "It's not important. I promise to leave you alone and not bother you again. Be safe."

She turned and walked away, and he had a mad urge to yell for her to come back.

"Hey, hun, did you want me for anything?" Monica asked in a testy tone.

He looked at her. "Sorry. I just wanted to see how you were doing?"

Monica scowled. "That's it?"

"Yeah, someone told me you'd gotten hurt." It was the first thing he could think of to say. He didn't want her to think he was interested in her.

"Hurt? No, I haven't been hurt," she said.

"Oh, hell. It must have been someone else they were talking about. I'm sorry."

Monica straightened away from him. He could see the disappointment on her face and felt like shit. "I'm glad you're okay."

She nodded. "Thanks. I better get back to work."

Dominik turned back to watch Tessa. His concern rose when he caught her rubbing her temples. She turned and walked out the door.

What the hell is she doing, leaving alone like that? He stood to follow her. He was a few feet from the door when one of her friends grabbed onto his arm to stop him.

"Dominik. Wait. I need to talk to you," Michelle said.

"Later. I want to make sure she gets home."

"Nicole was waiting outside for her, so she's not alone."

Dominik sighed in frustration but turned to face Michelle. "What do you need?"

"I need you to stop messing with Tessa. You're tearing her apart, and she is still dealing with the attack."

"I'm not trying to mess with her. I just want to make sure she's safe."

"Showing you care and then pushing her away is doing her more harm. She's been through enough. Her life has mostly sucked," Michelle said.

His eyes narrowed. "What does that mean?"

Michelle looked away and then turned back. "I can't tell you much, but I can tell you her whole life has been a struggle. She was finally starting to believe she could be happy. After the attack, her pain reminded me of her in college. I don't want her to go through that again. And she will if you keep messing with her emotions."

His stomach tensed. "Why did she have such a hard time? Didn't her family help her?"

Michelle looked confused. "What family?"

"Her family. Her parents and any siblings she might have?"

Michelle looked even more upset. "Is that what you think?"

"Yeah. I assumed she grew up somewhere in the suburbs," he said.

Michelle shook her head. "That's what's holding you back?"

"No, but it's the most important one." He waited for the woman to talk. He wanted to shake her, and then she stood in silence. "Tell me."

Michelle sighed. "I won't tell you all of it, but I will tell you there was no family."

He was shocked. "What?"

"She's never had a family. Her mother set her on church steps when she was a few days old and then left."

God, the thought of that beautiful woman going through that made him sick. "Why wasn't she adopted?"

"She was addicted to heroin, so she had to go through detox but then had some health issues that families didn't want to deal with. She went from foster home to foster home."

Oh, fuck. He didn't want to think she'd had it worse than him, but she did. At least he had some stability, being able to stay in one apartment his whole childhood.

"What else?" he asked.

Michelle shook her head. "I won't say anymore. It's her story to tell. Now, tell me, what else is keeping you away from her?"

"One is our size difference. I'm twice her size, for God's sake."

"Maybe, does that mean you'd hurt her somehow?" Michelle asked.

"Fuck, no. I'd never hurt her."

"Then I don't see the problem. Will it bother you if people stare when you are together?"

"I don't fucking care about that shit. I don't want her to feel embarrassed or sad because of it."

Michelle snorted. "I wouldn't worry about that, Dominik. She hasn't cared about what anyone thought as long as I've known her. What else?"

"I'm afraid I'll scare her."

"How?" she asked.

"I'm a very dominant man, both in bed and out."

"Once again, would you ever hurt her?"

"No!"

"Would you ever become a stalker and forbid her to see people or shit like that?"

"No. I will want to know if she's safe, though."

Michelle smiled. "That's a good thing, and it's something she needs."

"What if she can't handle me … you know … in bed?" Jesus, he couldn't believe he was asking her this.

"Do you know what I think?" she asked.

"What?"

"I think if there are things that bother either of

you, you'll be able to talk it out and compromise."

Fuck. Could it be that easy? "It would destroy me if she left me."

Michelle patted his arm. "I have to tell you about the first time she saw you. I've never seen a person fall for someone within a minute. She told me it felt like you were her other half. She'd say stuff like that every time she saw you."

Dominik swallowed and ran his hand through his hair. "Holy hell."

"What?"

"I felt the same way," he said.

Michelle smiled brightly. "My advice is to stop being a pussy and go get your woman. And stop thinking about the what ifs."

God, it felt like he could finally take a deep breath since he first saw her. The ball of anger disintegrated, and he felt good.

"I'm going to get her now."

"Good. It's about time. Oh, by the way, if you hurt her, I'll cut off your cock and shove it down your throat."

His head snapped back. "Jesus, woman. I didn't know you were so violent."

She smiled. "Well, now you do."

He hugged her and walked out the door. He needed to get to his angel as quickly as he could. Only when he had her in his arms would he feel whole.

LILA FOX

Chapter Five

Tessa waved goodbye to her friend Nicole before she closed and locked the door. Although new locks had been installed, she had a locksmith do another one. She needed all she could get to feel safe enough in her own home. It would have been better if they caught the guy, but until then, she'd do what she could. She walked around to all the windows and made sure the short pieces of pole she'd jammed in were still there and hadn't fallen out.

Her headache was slowly getting worse, so she took a couple of aspirins before she started the water in the bathtub. She dropped some lavender bath salts in, which always relaxed her, and pulled her hair into a messy bun. When the water level was high enough, she undressed and slid in.

Tessa rested her head against the bath pillow and closed her eyes. The instant relief she felt made her sigh. She felt her headache diminish and her body relax.

She thought about the previous hours and felt tears fill her eyes. She sniffed and then shook her head.

She had to get it into her mind and come to grips with the fact that she'd never have Dominik. He might be attracted to her but not enough to want to be with her. Tessa thought about the woman, Monica, who wrapped herself around him. She had to admit the woman probably fitted him better than she could. That woman had shoulder-length red hair, was about four inches taller than her, and had a great body. To top it off, she was beautiful.

Tessa was blonde, and her eyes were light blue. Her body was tiny compared to the other woman, and she didn't have nearly the size boobs she did. Tessa knew she paled in comparison to Monica.

Tessa turned her mind to the things she wanted to do around the house and in the backyard. Anything to keep her mind off him. She'd had all sorts of ideas but hadn't taken the time to start another project. Now was the perfect time. It would give her something to think about besides Dominik. She also planned on not going to the bar again. Maybe ever. She'd have her girlfriends come to her house and eat dinner, maybe play games, or sit around and drink wine and talk.

Tessa's eyes popped open when she heard someone at her front door, and she sat up so quickly the water went over the side of the tub. Who the hell would be at her door?

The knock came again, only harder. Her fear started to rise. She logically knew if it was the bad guy he probably wouldn't knock, but it didn't matter. She'd been scared for so long it was hard to stop.

The knock came a third time, making her get out of the bathtub and pull on her robe. She also grabbed the wasp spray on her way to the door. She peeked out the side window and almost dropped the can.

What in the world was Dominik doing there? God, how was she going to get over him when he kept doing this stuff?

"Baby, open the door," he said.

She shook her head but knew he couldn't see it.

"Sweetheart, I'll stand out here until you open the door. The neighbors will start to stare."

She gritted her teeth. "What do you want, Dominik?"

"I want to talk to you."

"You should go back to your date. We've got nothing more to say to each other."

She heard him sigh.

"She wasn't my date. I used her to push you away."

"It worked. Now, why are you tormenting me?"

"Let me in so we can talk," he pleaded.

Tears started to slide down her face. "I can't do this anymore."

"Me either. That's why we have to talk," he said. "Open the door."

"What else is there to say?"

"Sweetheart, open the door, or people are going to start calling the police."

Tessa set the spray off to the side and wiped her eyes before unlocking the door and cracking it open. She clutched her robe in one hand to keep it from opening.

"Tell me here," she said.

"No. I want to see your face."

"I'm not dressed. Let me get some clothes on, and then I'll come outside," she told him.

He flattened his hand against the door and started to inch it in until there was enough room for him to get through.

"Dominik. No. Please leave." She hated the tears that kept coming. "Please," she begged. "Or at least let me get dressed."

She could tell how upset he was seeing her crying.

"Baby, you're fine the way you are. I've seen you mostly naked. Remember?"

She nodded and bit down on her lip. "That was under unusual circumstances."

"It doesn't matter." He crossed his arms over his chest.

Tessa moved to the other side of the sofa, putting space between them. "What do you need to say?"

His scowl darkened, but at no time was she afraid of him. "You've been crying," he stated.

She almost laughed. "Yes. I do that when I'm upset."

"I'm sorry."

She frowned in confusion. "For what?"

"For being an ass and not giving us a chance."

Her mouth dropped open. "Where is this coming from?"

"It physically hurt when you walked away. It always did, but it's getting worse. I was on my way to follow you to make sure you got home when Michelle stopped me. She helped me get my head out of my ass."

Her hands tightened on her robe. "I don't understand."

"I'm not going to fight my attraction anymore."

"Why have you kept me away?" she asked.

"Because I was afraid you'd eventually leave me when you found out about my personality and where I came from."

"You had a mother, right?"

He nodded. "Yes. I also found out you didn't have anyone."

She felt a spear of pain piercing her heart before she nodded. "Michelle told you?"

"Yes."

"How much did she tell you?" she asked.

He dropped his arms and took a step toward her. "Not a lot. She said it was your story to tell. She just wanted to enlighten me about your childhood, so I'd get that thought of you having the perfect family out of my head, and I'd understand you better."

She nodded. "Tell me about the other thing."

"If you haven't guessed yet, I'm kind of a dominant man. There are things I'd need from you that you might not be willing to do."

"Like what?"

"I'd want you to obey me about certain things."

"Like what?" she asked again.

"There are several things. Like I'd want to know where you're at, I'd want to make sure you're safe and healthy, so I'd make sure you eat and get enough rest. I'd want to open doors for you."

"Why would you think I'd hate that?" she asked.

"Because my girlfriends before always did. They'd call me a Neanderthal and bitch that I was being too controlling."

She shrugged. "I don't have a problem with that. It just shows you care."

"There's also the bedroom."

A shiver skated up her spine. "What about it?"

"I'd want total submission from you."

That kind of freaked her out. "You wouldn't hurt me, right?"

His face darkened. "Fuck, no. I'd rather have my right arm cut off than hurt you."

"Then give me an example," she said.

"If I told you to strip and lay on the bed, you would do that instantly. I'd want to own you." He cursed under his breath. "That sounded bad. I'd want to be able to touch any part of your body at any time."

"I think I can handle that, but can we talk about the things that make me nervous?"

"Hell, yes. Our relationship would have total honesty. If you don't like something, tell me. I'm not opposed to compromise. We will talk about everything. We'll get to know each other better than the average couple."

"What happens if I do something wrong?"

He smiled. "I'll spank your ass. Not enough to hurt, but you'll feel the sting."

Her eyes widened, and her mouth dropped open.

"But … I'm not a child."

"No. You'll be my submissive."

She thought about it for a moment and then nodded. "Then I'm okay."

"If we take this step, you're mine for the rest of our lives."

Her heart skipped a beat. "That sounds serious, like a marriage."

"What we'll have is deeper than a regular marriage, although eventually, we'll get married."

She sucked in a breath. "All right."

"I won't let you go, but I promise to make you happier than you ever thought possible."

The tense feeling in her gut relaxed, allowing her to take a deep, cleansing breath. "Okay. I'll also try to make you happy."

"I already know that."

She smiled. She was already happier than she'd ever been.

Chapter Six

Dominik studied her intently. When she smiled, he felt like he could conquer the world. Now, he needed to touch her in any way. He needed to feel her close.

"Now, you have a choice. We can either watch a movie, go to sleep, or make love. I'll warn you that from this time forward, we'll never sleep one night apart."

He watched a flush of desire blanket her face.

"I want you."

"Then you'll have me." He stalked toward her and lifted her into his arms before he turned and took her into the bedroom. He laid her on the mattress and stripped off her robe.

He shook his head when she went to cover herself. "No, Angel, don't ever cover yourself with me."

She looked confused. "Angel?"

He grinned as he unbuttoned his shirt. "The first time I saw you, I thought you were an angel, so I've called you my angel since."

He could tell that pleased her.

He finished undressing and stood still to let her look at him. He didn't like the apprehension he saw on her face. He felt his heart drop. "Are the scars bothering you?"

Her eyes widened. "God, no. It's…" She pointed to his penis.

"We'll fit just fine," he told her as he stroked his cock.

"It's just … I mean, I know we're not close to the same height, but I hadn't thought about you being big everywhere. I just don't know if I can…"

He lay down beside her and cradled her face. "Don't. I promise we'll fit. I plan to take all the time you need tonight. You just have to trust me."

Her fingers skimmed over his cheek. "I do. I trust you more than anyone."

"That makes me very happy, Angel. Now, relax, and let me make you feel good."

Dominik started by kissing her, softly at first, but then deepening the contact, the hotter her desire got. At the same time, he let his hand drift down to cup one of her breasts. He tormented both her nipples until they were hard little pebbles and a deep red.

Tessa was already begging, and he hadn't touched her cunt yet. He let his fingers skim over her skin, getting closer to the place he knew she needed him the most.

The longer he held out, her need would grow and become frantic. When he saw her tears of frustration, he knew she was ready for his finger.

He lifted his head. "Angel, are you on birth control?"

She panted and then nodded. "Yes."

"I haven't been with a woman in years. Do you trust me to go without a condom?"

"Yes. I trust you. I'd rather feel your skin against mine than rubber."

He smiled. "I feel the same way." His head dipped, and he continued to kiss her.

When his hand got to the junction of her thighs, one of his fingers pressed in between her cunt lips and down on her clit. She screamed and arched off the mattress. Fuck, she was perfect. He'd hardly touched her, and she was ready to go off.

"Let's see how tight you are," he murmured before slipping one of his fingers into her cunt.

They both groaned. She begged and pleaded, which told him she was ready for a deeper touch.

She was tighter than anything he'd ever felt, and

he was starting to worry that they *would* have trouble fitting together. Hell, there was no way he was going to stop. He'd dreamed about this for months. He would work hard to stay in control so he didn't hurt her.

"Here, Angel, let me get two fingers into you."

When he got them in, he started to scissor them, stretching her. When he felt she was lost in her desire enough, he pushed in three.

A jagged edge of passion started to build in him, so he bit down on his lip hard to keep himself centered and under control. Her need was growing, but he wanted her frantic before he started to fuck her. He worked his fingers inside of her and slowed down a bit because she was taking them easier.

"God, Dominik. Please," she begged repeatedly.

"I'll take care of you. Just relax, Angel."

Her head started to thrash back and forth, and her nails dug into his arm. She was so close, but he wouldn't get in her until he was one hundred percent sure she was ready for him.

"Please, God, Dominik."

"I know. Relax for me." He mounted her, making sure to keep most of the weight off her with his elbows. He reached between them and lined his cock up to her cunt. He pushed the head in and then stopped.

"Tell me if anything hurts, Angel."

She nodded.

Dominik started to push into her slowly, inch by inch. It took a while because he took his time, but he was finally able to bottom out in her cunt. "There, Baby, you took all of me."

He almost smiled when he saw her look of concentration. He wiped a drop of sweat from the side of his face with his shoulder. Sweat had also pooled in the base of his spine, and his body was rigid with the control of holding himself back from pounding into her like it demanded.

His cock slid in and out of her with a slow steady slide. He was able to keep that up for a minute until she started to beg him, and her cunt tightened on him. He was relieved because he knew he was so close to losing it, and he wanted to make sure she came first.

"Come for me, Angel."

He hissed when her cunt clamped down on his cock and she screamed out, blending with his groan and filing the room with their satisfaction.

Dominik rested his head against her shoulder as he fought to get control of his heart and breathing. He'd never felt this close to a person in his life, and it unsettled him a bit. Oh, he'd known she was special, but this went so far beyond that.

He rolled them to the side and held her tightly against his chest, keeping his cock deep inside of her. He listened to her breath calming, then evening out, before it deepened, telling him she'd fallen asleep.

He gently pulled out of her and just held her for another moment before he carefully lifted her onto the pillow and slid out of bed. He pissed and then pulled on his boxers before getting a warm, wet cloth. He took it back to her and carefully lifted one of her legs and then wiped the cum and sweat from her cunt.

After, he threw the cloth to the hamper and covered her with a blanket before going into the kitchen. He found and pulled down a glass and filled it with water. He drank deeply as he stood looking out the kitchen window. His thoughts circled in his head, and he was unable to pick just one.

He decided he'd take some time when he was alone to get a grip on his emotions. At the moment, he wanted to be back in bed with her.

Dominik arranged her on her side with her back against his chest and pulled the blanket over them. He kissed the back of her head, closed his eyes, and slept.

LILA FOX

Chapter Seven

Tessa stayed as still as she could and concentrated on pretending to be asleep. She fought the tears that burned her eyes when he got out of bed. Without looking at him she could feel his turmoil and she didn't know what to do.

She lay still as he wiped her clean and then listened as he walked out of the room. She moved to her back and stared at the ceiling. What was she supposed to do? Question him or give him space? She'd never been in this position in her life.

After several minutes, she heard his footsteps coming back. She rolled to her side again, and closed her eyes. She heard him turn off the lights, and then she felt him slide into bed behind her. It caught her by surprise. She had really thought he'd make an excuse and leave.

He circled her waist with an arm and tightened it to press her tight against him. It took so much effort to pretend to be asleep and not burst into tears. It seemed to take forever for his breathing to slow and deepen. When she was sure he was asleep, she let the tears come.

She cried silently until she was exhausted and used the blanket to wipe her eyes and nose. Should she get up? The thought of leaving him was physically painful. What if this was the only night she'd have with him? She didn't want to give it up. She wanted to soak up any affection he gave her, even if it was for only one night.

How would she face him in the morning? God, the thought of having to say goodbye made jagged pain fill her chest and twist her stomach.

Tessa lay there and finally fell asleep but woke every time he moved, afraid he was going to leave. When the sunlight started to rise, she was wiped out and had given up on sleep. She carefully slid out from under his arm and off the bed. She carefully closed the bathroom door. She put her hair up and jumped into the shower, washing herself quickly.

After drying off and brushing her teeth, she silently opened the bathroom door and walked into her closet. She pulled on socks, underwear, old jeans, and a t-shirt. When she was dressed, she walked into the kitchen and started the coffeemaker.

She was sipping her first cup when she felt the energy in the room change, telling her Dominik stood behind her.

"Good morning," she said without turning. "Do you have time for a cup of coffee?"

When she didn't hear anything, she turned and swallowed nervously. This huge, magnificent specimen of a man leaned against the doorjamb with his arms crossed, wearing only his jeans, which he hadn't zipped yet. Her eyes couldn't stop scanning him. Seeing him without clothing showed how muscular he was. Every muscle stood out sharply. His biceps alone were as large as her waist, and his legs were like tree trunks. There was not a bit of fat on the man. The tendons on his arms and hands also showed how truly strong he was. The thought of those hands on her body made her cunt spasm. He was so … everything. She loved everything about him.

His eyes narrowed on her. "Are you kicking me out?"

She swallowed and shook her head. "No. I just thought…"

He tilted his head to the side. "Thought what?"

She looked away. "That you'd have to leave."

"Look at me, Angel."

She had to swallow a few times to hold back the

tears that burned her eyes.

"Now," he demanded.

She braced herself when he stepped closer, cupped her chin in his hand, and raised her head. Tessa wanted more than anything to wrap her arms around him and never let go, but she cared too much to try to be conniving and make him feel guilty.

"Tell me what's wrong," he murmured gently.

His tone almost made her lose control.

"Last night after…"

"After we made love?" he asked.

Tessa nodded. "I sensed that you were very uncomfortable. I've had to read and feel the emotions of people around me my whole life, so I'm pretty good at it. I don't think you want to be here, and I … I understand."

He didn't release her face and stared down at her for a long minute. "I don't."

Her brows pinched together. "Don't what?" she asked when he stalled.

"I don't want to leave. In fact, if I had my way, we'd be together every minute except when we're working. The only thing that's going to change my mind is if you can't stand to be with me. Even then, I'll do whatever I need to change your mind."

Her stomach settled a bit. "But you were unsettled, right?"

He nodded. "Yeah, but not for the reason you think."

Her hand, which was not holding the cup, gripped his thick wrist. "Then why?"

"Everything I feel for you is exponentially more and deeper than I've ever felt in my life. When I was inside your sweet body, I never wanted to leave. It took an amazing amount of effort to pull out of you. The magnitude of emotion surprised me. I never thought I could care about someone as much as I love you."

She couldn't hold back the tears from falling. This time it was in relief. "I feel the same way."

His thumb slid over her cheek before he took the cup from her, put it to the side, lifted her, and set her on the counter. His hand slid to the back of her head and controlled her as his face descended. The kiss made them both moan. Her arms crept around his neck, and she widened her legs to pull him closer to her.

She wanted to beg him to strip her and get as deep as he could inside her. "Please."

He raised his head and studied her. "I want to make sure you're okay to take me right now. Last night, I knew you felt some discomfort. You've got to be sore."

She shook her head. "It wasn't discomfort, I felt stretched, and it might have stung a bit to begin with, but you had me so hot and needy, it almost added to the desire I was feeling."

Heat flared in his eyes. "So, you liked the bit of pain I gave you?"

She bit her lip, felt her face heat with a blush, and nodded.

He smiled at her so gently. "I think you're perfect in every way, and then you do something to make me feel like I'm a god," he said and chuckled.

She smiled. "To me, you are," she said sincerely.

She squealed when he lifted her, threw her over his shoulder, and walked into the bedroom. He carefully laid her on her back and stripped her clothing off. Within a minute, she was naked and watching him yank his jeans down and off.

He came down on top of her, careful not to smother her, and started kissing her again.

It seemed to go on and on. She begged him and was ready to yell when his hand slid down and cupped her breast.

"We've got to work on your patience, Angel."

"Yeah, okay. But later."

He smirked and let his hand glide farther down until he was between her thighs. One of his fingers speared into her, making her scream and arch under him. Jesus, just his finger was enough to send her over. When she got close, he always stopped.

"Oh, Sweetheart. You're so fucking juicy."

She nodded.

"This tells me how much you need me," he said against her lips.

She nodded again. "Please."

She felt him lift himself a bit and then felt him start to press his cock into her tight sheath. She thought she heard herself ask him for more because he was going too slow, but his expression didn't change, and neither did his penetration.

He was halfway in and stopped. "How are you doing, Angel? Are you sore at all?"

Tessa shook her head. "No. The only discomfort I feel is because you're holding back, and I need you as deep as you can go."

Without another word, he lunged into her. His cock was embedded in her now, and he didn't pause but started to fuck her with hard, fast, powerful thrusts.

She felt herself tighten on him, and then her world spiraled around her as wave upon wave of euphoria consumed her. He didn't allow her to come down but sent her over again. The strength of that orgasm seemed stronger than the previous one. Her lungs pumped air in and out, and her heart raced in her chest.

"One more time," he said.

Her eyes widened. "No. I can't."

Dominik gritted his teeth. "The hell you can't."

She thought he'd been hard on her, which is what she needed. But his cock pistoned in and out of her with such force, she would have scooted up the mattress if he didn't have a grip on the back of her neck.

He held her steady, not giving her any mercy. She felt him reach between them and then screamed when he pressed down on her clit. She flew and didn't think she'd ever feel anything as crazy and wonderful as the orgasm he was pushing on her. She heard him grunt and then moan before she felt his cum fill her up and trickle out of her.

They both lay still and concentrated on calming their hearts.

She was barely lucid when he pressed his mouth to her ear.

"Never ever doubt that I want you, Angel. You are already a part of my soul."

She blinked as tears filled her eyes. "I feel the same way."

An hour ago, she thought she'd lose him and now they were so much a part of each other, she knew they'd be together forever.

Chapter Eight

Dominik kissed her forehead. "How about we get up? I'd like you to pack some outfits, and we also need to go to the store today."

Tessa looked up at him in confusion. "Why pack?"

"Because we're staying at my house from now on."

She lifted to her elbow. "Why?"

He let his fingers skate up and down her back. "Because I'll become broken and twisted if I have to sleep in this bed again, and my house has great security, which will make you safer."

He watched as she thought about it for a moment and then relaxed when she nodded. "Okay."

"How about you go get dressed?"

Her nose wrinkled. "I should shower…"

He shook his head. "No, I want you to smell like me all day."

She smiled and blushed at the same time.

He liked the excitement that burst from her. "Go. Get packed. I'll shower, and then we'll be ready to go. I want us to stop somewhere and get breakfast."

"I'd like that. I'm very hungry."

He didn't want to bring up the fact that she still hadn't regained the weight she'd lost after the attack. He knew the reminder would dull her happiness, and that was the last thing he wanted. Within twenty minutes, they were heading toward a diner that had great food.

"Coffee?" the waitress said after they sat down.

They both nodded. She set down cups and filled them. "I'll be back to get your order."

"Thank you," Tessa said.

He reached for the menu the woman handed him and glanced at the vast selection. When he decided, he set the menu to the side and took a sip from his coffee cup.

Dominik reached across the table and took one of her hands. "Is there anything you need to get done today?"

"I was planning on cleaning my house, but that's not important. It doesn't really need it. It's just routine to clean every Saturday."

He nodded. "I should stop by one of my construction sites. Although I trust my foremen, I still like to check in at least once a week."

"That would be nice. I'd like to see what you do."

The waitress interrupted them and took their order. "I'll get that out to you."

"Thank you," both said.

"Did you always want to be a nurse?" he asked her. He had wanted to ask about her childhood but decided to do that when they were home. Knowing her life had been so hard bothered him more than he thought.

She nodded. "Yes. I had a lot of medical issues when I was young, and the nurses were always so good to me. I want to be able to give that to children because it makes a difference."

"You're pretty special, you know that?" he told her. He smiled when she blushed.

She shook her head. "Not really. Oh, I try to be the best nurse I can be, but there is always room for improvement."

"That's with anyone. I never stop reading and learning about new innovations or tools I could use."

"What made you want to be in construction?" she asked.

"I started working for a guy when I was fourteen."

Her eyes widened. "Fourteen?"

He nodded. "Yeah, my mother was irresponsible and I spent some nights without food, or I grew out of my clothing and she never had any money for more so I got a job. That was the time I sprouted up, so I was going through clothes regularly."

"I think I stopped growing when I was eleven," she said and laughed.

"You're perfect the way you are," he said.

She rolled her eyes. "Are you sure you wouldn't want me to have a few more inches?"

He shook his head. "No, I wouldn't change anything about you."

They were interrupted when the waitress set their plates down. He grinned at Tessa's shocked look when four large plates were set in front of him.

"Is there anything else I can get you?" the waitress asked.

They both shook their heads.

"All right. I'll be back to check on you."

He looked at her plate. It had one egg, two pieces of toast, and a side of fruit. "Is that all you're eating?"

"I can't eat a lot at one time. It upsets my stomach."

He nodded and started in on his food and glanced up when he didn't see her move. "What?"

"You're really going to eat all of that?" she asked.

He reached for her hand again. "Angel, I'm six-five and two hundred seventy-five pounds. I have to eat a lot to maintain my body and give me energy. I work it off quickly."

"I'll have to quadruple every recipe," she said and grinned.

"Don't worry, I'll help you."

They both ate in silence for a few minutes.

Tessa finished and sat back, drinking her coffee.

He could tell she was relaxed as she stared out the window, waiting for him to finish.

Dominik wiped his mouth on a napkin and took a drink from his cup. "Do you want anything else, Angel?"

She turned and looked at him, smiling. "No. I'm good."

Dominik raised his hand to get the waitress's attention.

"How is everything?" the waitress asked.

"It was good. I want the bill, please," he said.

She pulled her pad out of her pocket, tore off his bill, and handed it to him. "Here you go," she said.

"Thank you," he said and pulled out his wallet. He threw several bills down, enough for the meal and a nice tip, before he stood and held his hand out to Tessa.

He wrapped his arm around her and led her out to the truck.

"Let me get you in," he said, lifting her into the seat and snapping on her seat belt.

When he pulled out of the parking lot, he took her hand. "Do you feel up for the grocery store, Angel?"

She turned and smiled at him. "Sure. I'd like you to finish your story about how you got into construction."

"I was lucky to find a guy that owned a construction business. Stan was an old gruff guy, but he knew what he was doing and taught me everything. I worked after school every day and every weekend. It not only made me money, but it was a step toward my future and kept me out of trouble like most of my friends did. A lot of them ended up in jail or worse, dead."

She squeezed his hand. "I'm sorry."

Dominik shrugged. "It was the life I'd been born into. I'm afraid I would have ended up like them if it hadn't been for Stan. He kept me focused and didn't let me skirt on schoolwork. He told me I needed to get as smart as I could if I ever wanted to take over his business."

"Oh, wow. I'm so glad you found him."

"Me, too. I graduated early and took business college courses while I worked with him full time."

"God, you were so young to be so driven."

He shook his head. "No. I was determined to break the cycle of poverty my family had always been in, and I knew this was my only chance."

"When I was twenty-two, Stan had a heart attack. He survived, but the doctor told him he couldn't work again if he wanted to live. I took over the whole business. I'd been managing different sites already, but being responsible for everything was terrifying. The last thing I wanted to do was disappoint him."

"You were so young. How did the older guys deal with that?"

He shot her a grin. "At first, I got a lot of shit, but it helped that I was going to college, and my size helped, too. There were a few times when some guy pushed me or would pick fights, but all it took was me to lay him flat with one blow. The few I wanted to keep, I gave them the opportunity to stay, but if they didn't give it their all and respect me, they'd be gone."

He remembered the first year after taking over had been hard. He'd had to outwork everyone and put in twice the hours. He was lucky he still had Stan around to answer questions.

"I'm assuming he's gone?"

Dominik nodded. "Yeah, I was twenty-four."

"I'm sorry," she said.

Dominik had been thankful for being with him at the end, so he wasn't alone. The old guy never married or had kids, so he considered Dominik his son and left everything to him after he passed. He'd been surprised when he realized that not only was the business worth a few million dollars, but the old guy had left him his house, where he lived now, and several million dollars in stocks and IRAs.

Dominik knew he never had to work another day in his life, but he continued like he'd been doing because he'd always felt Stan looking down from Heaven, and he still wanted to make him proud.

"When I was twenty-eight, I changed the name of the business. People were confused that I was the owner and not a Kenova, which Stan was. It made things easier."

"I bet Stan's so proud of you."

Dominik smiled. "I always have him in mind, and I still feel he's part of my life."

Stan had always told him if he worked hard enough, he could accomplish and get everything he'd ever dreamed of, and he was right.

Chapter Nine

Tessa couldn't get the smile off her face as they drove to Dominik's. She'd had so much fun with him at the grocery store and loved that he had a hand on her most of the time.

They turned down a street she'd never been to, making her sit up and look around. The houses were bigger in this part of town, and each sat on an acre or more of land.

Her eyes widened when he drove to the end of the road and turned into a long driveway. Her eyes darted around as she tried to take in everything. The land was left natural, but when the house came into view, she saw the yard around it was lush grass, and several trees and bushes were scattered about.

The house itself was large, two stories high, and had a wraparound porch. It was made of rock on the bottom and stained wood on the top floor. It fit in perfectly with the natural surroundings.

She hadn't realized they'd stopped until her door opened. She looked at Dominik. "Your house is amazing."

Dominik looked around. "Stan left this to me after he passed. I've done some renovations, but I wanted to keep it as close as possible to how he had it."

He unsnapped her and lifted her to the ground. Before she took another step, he had his arms wrapped around her and held her tightly against his chest.

"I've imagined you here so many times, Angel. I never thought it would happen." He tipped her head up. "The feeling is better than I ever imagined." He bent and pressed his lips to hers.

Tessa wrapped her arms around his waist and

gave herself over to him. She had no idea how much time passed before Dominik lifted his head.

"As much as I'd like to lay you down and fuck you blind, we have frozen food we need to take care of."

She was disappointed but understood. He released her. "Go up to the porch. I'll grab some of the bags."

"I can help."

He shook his head. "No, I've got it."

"I can at least take my bag. It's not heavy at all."

He looked like he was going to say no, but then just nodded. "That's fine."

He followed her up the stairs and stood off to the side while he unlocked the door. He motioned her in first and then followed.

"The kitchen is back here, Angel."

She set down her bag and followed. Dominik had set the bags down on the counter.

"I'll be right back," he said.

Tessa started to unload the bags and set everything in groups. He came back and dropped more bags down.

He came back the third time. "This is it."

She grinned. "I would hope so. Is there going to be enough room in the refrigerator and cupboards for this?"

He chuckled. "We'll figure it out."

"Where does everything go?" she asked.

He opened a few of the top cupboards. "I shove what I can in here, and there's also a pantry right there," he said and pointed at a smaller-sized door.

She walked over and opened it, finding it so cluttered she knew she would never be able to find anything. It was bigger than she expected, but she knew if something wasn't done, she'd never use it.

He must have caught her look of dismay because

he just pulled her into his arms.

"Angel, I want you to arrange this any way you want. I didn't know how to organize it, so I tossed shit everywhere. We also have a freezer on the back porch."

She glanced at the refrigerator/freezer in the kitchen and had never seen one so large. "Are you sure you don't mind?"

He laughed. "Mind? Hell, no. I'd appreciate you taking over. I'm afraid you'll find cans that expired years ago because I didn't know they were here."

"Put the frozen things in the freezer in the back. I'll organize that last," she said.

He grabbed the things and walked off. By the time he got back, she had cleared out a few of the cupboards and set the things on the kitchen table to be sorted.

She glanced over to see his expression of dismay and laughed.

"Are you sure you want to deal with this?" he asked.

"You're going to think I'm weird, but I love organizing."

He smirked. "Yeah, that's a bit weird, but thank God you do."

She smacked his arm as she passed him for more things.

"Is there anything I can do to help?"

She looked at his expression and had to bite her lip to keep from laughing at the confusion and dismay on his face. "No, I'd like to do it myself. Do you have work to do?"

"Hell, yeah, there's always paperwork to do and things around the house to get done."

"Then go do that. I'll work in here and make a quick lunch in a few hours for us."

"This is going to take you a week to do," he said.

She snorted. "No. I'll have the majority done today."

He shook his head. "I'll get out of your hair. If you need me, yell. My office is down the hallway and to the left."

"I will."

She turned to get to work but gasped when he tugged her against him, turned her head, and kissed her until she was breathless. He released her and then chuckled.

She scowled because she knew he was teasing her. "Go," she said. "Or I'll never get anything done."

She heard him chuckle as he walked away and couldn't help but smile.

Tessa cleared everything out of the pantry and cabinets. There was so much that she'd had to set things on chairs and even the floor. She already had a pile of expired food. She also unloaded the rest of the top cabinets and decided to work on the bottom ones later.

She filled the sink with soapy water and climbed onto the counter to wipe the cupboards out. She bit back a scream when she felt hands grab her waist.

"What the hell do you think you're doing?" Dominik growled.

She looked over her shoulder at him. "Cleaning."

"No. Why are you kneeling on the counter?"

"Because I couldn't reach."

He closed his eyes before he lifted her and set her on her feet. "Angel, I don't want you to put yourself in danger."

She almost snorted but didn't want to upset him more than he already was. "I was being careful."

He gripped her shoulders. "It doesn't matter. You need to call me if you need something up high."

"I didn't want to bother you," she told him.

"You're never a bother. My main job in life is to keep you happy and safe."

She didn't like that he thought her so weak she couldn't clean without him.

"I can see from the look on your face that you don't agree, but please let me do that. I know we'll disagree on things, but I want us to talk them out. I can compromise on some things. Your safety isn't one of them."

She sighed and nodded.

"Good girl, now tell me what you need."

She explained what she wanted and concentrated on wiping the shelves down in the pantry. The food closet looked a lot bigger empty than when things were shoved in.

"Do you need anything else, Angel?"

She turned to him and shook her head. "No, are you hungry yet?"

"Yeah, but let me help." He started to pull things from the refrigerator. "I don't want to go to the site today. I talked to my foreman. I told him I'd stop by in the next few days."

"I hope you're not going because of me."

He shook his head. "No. I've got a lot of paperwork to do, and I want to spend time with you."

He put everything down as she made some space at the kitchen table.

She set plates and silverware down and then went back for glasses. "What do you want to drink?" she asked.

"I'll take a beer."

She came back with a can for him and a glass of water for herself.

Tessa studied him as they ate, and she couldn't get over how much he turned her on. Her whole body felt alive when he was around. It was something she'd never heard of before meeting him.

The thought of not having him in her life flashed through her mind, and she fought to keep the desolate expression off her face. She just had to pray nothing would ever happen to take him from her.

Chapter Ten

Tessa stood near her desk on the floor of the hospital where she worked. She kept glancing at the time, counting down the minutes until she could be with Dominik again.

She sighed in exasperation when she felt a body press up against her side. She knew exactly who it was without looking because of the strong cologne he always wore.

She took a step to the side. "Dr. Farley, how many times have I asked you not to get so close to me?"

The young doctor chuckled and tried to put his hand on her shoulder, only to have her knock it off and scowl at him.

"Come on, Tessa. I know I can make you happy if you only give us a chance."

"I've told you I'm in a committed relationship, and there's no way I'd jeopardize it. Especially for some guy that sleeps with more people in a month than I have my whole life."

He rolled his eyes. "I'm just gaining experience. It will make what I can do for you seem magical."

She snorted. "I think you need to back off. If my man finds out you're trying to touch me, he'll wipe the floor with you."

"Oh, come on. For one thing, he doesn't have to know, and for the other, I'm a pretty big guy. I'm not afraid."

"You should be," a deep, dark voice said behind them.

Both turned abruptly. Tessa relaxed, smiled, and walked to him when he held his hand out to her.

"Who the fuck are you?" the doctor asked.

"Right now, I'm your worst nightmare." Dominik looked at her, his eyes scanning her. "Angel, I want you to go and get your things and meet me by the elevator."

She paused for a moment.

Dominik ran his thumb over her cheek. "Go, Angel. We'll discuss this later at home."

Tessa lay her hand on his chest. "You can't kill him, Dominik."

Dominik smirked. "I probably won't, but I need to have a private talk with him."

She nodded, and without looking back at the doctor, she walked into the nurses' lounge and pulled the things from her locker. She walked out of the room and glanced back down the hallway to see Dominik standing very close to the doctor, and she saw the fear in the man's face. Good, he needed to realize that he couldn't sexually harass every woman he wanted.

Tessa stood by the elevator and waited. Within five minutes, Dominik was striding toward her with his eyes narrowed. If she didn't know him as well as she did, she might have been nervous, but she knew without a doubt he'd never hurt her.

Dominik wrapped his arm around her waist and pushed the elevator button. Neither said anything as they stepped in. An older woman was already there and smiled at them. Tessa leaned her head against Dominik's chest. She felt his hand cup her face and lift it before he kissed her gently.

"Oh, my. If I might say, you two look so good together," she said. "My husband was much larger than me, and I remember the looks we sometimes got, but I wouldn't have changed anything about him."

Tessa smiled at the woman. "Thank you."

"You'll make beautiful children."

Tessa felt Dominik stiffen, but he stayed silent.

"I'd like to think so," Tessa said.

The elevator doors slid open, and the woman stepped out. "You two take care."

Tessa raised her hand. "You, too."

When the doors slid closed, Tessa looked up at Dominik. The muscle in his jaw ticked, telling her he was more upset about the situation with the doctor than she had first thought.

"I'm sorry."

He glanced down at her. "For not telling me you were getting harassed?"

She sighed and nodded. "I thought I could handle it on my own. I know how busy you are right now, and I didn't want to disturb you with this."

"That's not your place, Angel. I'm the one who protects you, but I must know about these things so I can fix them. I can guarantee that man will never bother you again."

She kissed his chest. "I know I was wrong."

"We'll talk more about this when we get home."

She nodded and rested against him.

The ride home was silent, but Dominik kept hold of her hand, and his thumb rubbed back and forth on her knuckle. When they got home, Dominik came around, opened her door, unsnapped her seat belt, and lifted her out of the truck.

He took her hand and led her into the house. "Why don't you go and shower first?" he said.

She hoped he'd shower with her, but she didn't push him. She nodded. "Okay."

Tessa took her time, giving Dominik a chance to settle a bit more. When she walked out of the bedroom in her lounge pants and shirt, he was looking out at his backyard.

"I'm done," she said.

He turned, glanced at her, and nodded. "I'll be right back."

She watched him move around her and into the bedroom. Her heart sank when she realized he was more upset than she'd thought. Another thought popped into her head. She remembered when his body stiffened when the older lady mentioned children. It was one thing they hadn't talked about. Now that she thought about it, they really hadn't talked about the future at all.

He'd said he wanted them together forever a few times in the beginning but hadn't heard anything else in the four months she'd lived with him.

Tessa decided to start dinner. She'd try to get the courage to ask him some questions, but she didn't want to push too much now since he was already upset.

The chicken she'd thawed that morning was frying while she cut the potatoes into small chunks and then into a boiling pot of water. She checked the rolls she'd put in the oven to find them just about done.

She heard his footsteps behind her. "I hope you're hungry."

She glanced over her shoulder to see him pulling a beer from the refrigerator. When he didn't say anything, she turned back to the potatoes and concentrated on them. Within thirty minutes, the rolls were done, the chicken crisp and brown, and the potatoes mashed.

Nothing was said as Dominik set the table while she brought over the bowls and plates of food.

"Do you want another beer, Dominik?" she asked before she sat down.

He shook his head.

She'd rather have him yell at her than ignore her. Any appetite she had fled. She sat down and put a tiny bit of food on her plate. She tried to take a few bites, but every time, she'd have to take a drink of water to get it down her throat.

Tessa finally set her fork on her plate and stood. "I'm going to grab my book and read for a while. Leave everything here, and I'll get it later.

He grabbed onto her arm when she passed him. "Where do you think you're going? You hardly ate anything."

She looked away. "I'm not very hungry right now."

"Sit down, Angel," he murmured.

Tessa sighed and sat back in her chair. She refused to look at him and waited. When he didn't say anything for a few minutes, she'd had enough.

"Look. I'm sorry about the doctor. I promise to tell you from now on."

She wished he'd say something or even just look at her. She couldn't take this much longer before she burst into tears.

LILA FOX

Chapter Eleven

Dominik took a long drink of his beer. He was upset about the situation with the doctor and wanted to make sure she understood she was never to hold anything back from him again.

He understood her thoughts but didn't agree with them at all. He felt it was his duty to keep her safe and make her happy. He couldn't do that if he had no idea what was happening with her.

"I am disappointed you didn't tell me. You said you just didn't want to bother me, but you've got to know by now that nothing is more important than you," he said. "I need to know everything, or I don't feel like I'm doing my job."

"I don't want you to think I'm incapable," she said.

"It's not that at all. I know you've taken care of yourself for a long time, but I want you to let me do that now," he told her. "I want—no, I *need*—to know you're always okay. Especially since that bastard Pierce hasn't been caught yet."

"I'm always very careful. I don't leave my floor until you get there. If I have to, I make sure someone else is with me."

"Good. I need you to take every precaution."

She nodded.

Dominik watched her bite her lip, which told him there was something on her mind. "What's up?"

She looked at him. "The lady in the elevator."

"What about her?"

"I felt you stiffened when she talked about children."

He was afraid she'd bring this up.

"It's something we've never talked about," she said.

He leaned back, trying to think of a way out of the conversation.

"Do you not want them?" she asked when he didn't answer.

What could he say? He'd always dreamed of them, but he was terrified that her being pregnant with his child could kill her. There was no way she'd be able to carry a baby that was at least ten pounds, and then give birth to it. He'd been over thirteen pounds when he was born. His mother always bitched about what he did to her body and how he almost killed her.

"I haven't really thought about it."

Tessa looked at him suspiciously. "Never?"

He shrugged. "Not really. I don't think they're important for me."

He could tell it was upsetting her, but he didn't think he could stop. "Do you think you could stay with me without them?" he asked.

She looked down. "This is sudden. I don't know. I'd have to think about it."

"How about we deal with this later? We might not have to even think about it," he told her.

He could tell she took it the wrong way and hated the sorrow in her eyes. Before he could say anything else, she stood and took her plate to the sink.

"Angel?"

"What?" she asked without turning. "You're right. Why talk about something that might not pertain to us?"

"I think you're hearing me wrong," he said.

She shook her head. "No. I hear you just fine, and I agree."

He studied her when she came back to the table and grabbed more dishes. It broke his heart when she tried to smile and act like she wasn't hurting.

He reached for her, and she flinched.

She caught herself. "I'm sorry. I just want to get this cleaned up and go to bed."

Dominik looked at the clock on the wall. "It's only seven o'clock."

She had turned her back again. "Yes. But I'm tired, and I have a long day tomorrow."

His brows pinched together. "Why?"

"I was invited to go over to Michelle's after work for a girls' night."

"When were you going to say something to me?" he asked.

"I was going to tell you when you picked me up, but things got a bit crazy. It's not a big deal, is it?"

He stood and walked to her, standing very close. "Turn around, Angel. I don't like talking to the back of your head."

He saw her stiffen and then turned. His stomach tightened when he saw how blank her expression was. She was building a wall between them and didn't know what to do. His emotions had been in turmoil since learning she hadn't said anything to him about a man trying to touch her. It had gone downhill from there. He decided to give them some space and then bring it up later.

"No, it's fine. You'll ride home with her?"

Tessa nodded.

"What time do you think I can come and get you?" he asked.

"Oh, you don't have to do that. One of the girls can bring me home."

His face darkened. "No, I'll come and get you. Now, what time?"

"I think around nine, but I'll call you if the time

changes," she said.

He wasn't going to push her anymore. "That's fine. Let me help with the dishes."

She shook her head and turned back to face the sink. "No, I've got it. Go in and relax. This won't take me long."

He stood still for a moment before grabbing another beer from the refrigerator and walking out of the room. When he got to his office, he sat behind his desk and started his computer. He needed to get some paperwork done, or he'd get so far behind he'd be doing it all weekend, and he wanted to spend it with Tessa.

It took an immense amount of effort to keep his mind on work and not on Tessa. When he checked the time, he was shocked to see that three hours had passed. He turned off his computer, stood, and stretched before going to find Tessa.

All the lights were off except one in the hallway. When he opened the bedroom door, it was to see Tessa already in bed.

Dominik brushed his teeth and stripped off his clothing before sliding into bed behind her. He could tell she was sleeping deeply, so he carefully wrapped his body around her. When he checked and found her still asleep, he exhaled and relaxed.

He was disappointed that she hadn't come to say good night because he had wanted—no, needed—to fuck her until she knew she belonged to him, and that would never change. But he also understood why she hadn't.

He'd find time tomorrow to sit down and talk with her because he hated the wall between them. He would make sure she understood how much he loved her and was afraid for her to have his baby. If they didn't have a discussion, he was afraid the abyss would grow between them, and he might just lose her.

The thought made him furious and sick at the same time. If that happened, he'd never be the same.

LILA FOX

Chapter Twelve

Tessa found Michelle at the nurse's station the next day. "Hey, girl. Is there a chance we can get together after work?"

Michelle studied her. "Of course. What's going on?"

"Let's talk about that later. Okay?"

Michelle hugged her. "All right. I'll meet you in the lounge, and we'll go to my house. Is that okay?"

Tessa nodded. "Should we pick up some wine on the way there?"

"If it's okay, I'll have Nicole pick some up and meet us at my house. Is it all right that she's there?"

"Yes. That would be great. I need any advice I can get," Tessa said.

Michelle squeezed her arm. "I'll see you soon."

Tessa nodded and walked the other way. The next few hours seemed to drag. She knew part of it was lack of sleep, but also how miserable she felt about the discord in her relationship. When Dominik woke her in the middle of the night and made love to her, she felt herself relax, but when she felt the same turmoil from him when they got up the next morning, she grew anxious.

The ride to the hospital that morning was mostly in silence. It helped a bit that he still held her hand and kissed her breathlessly when they got to her floor, but not enough to keep the worry that things had changed between them and that they might not be able to go back to what it was.

When the shift change came, Tessa collected her things and waited for Michelle.

"I'm sorry," Michelle said as she hustled in.

"Don't be. We had many patients today," Tessa

said.

Michelle pulled out her bag. "I'm having David walk us to my car. It's just an extra precaution."

"That's fine."

The three talked as they walked out to the parking lot. David, the security guard, waited until they left before heading back into the hospital.

They stopped at the light. "I asked Nicole to pick up Chinese and the wine."

"That's sounds good," Tessa said. "I didn't get any time for lunch."

"Me either, and I'm starving."

They pulled up to Michelle's small house and walked in. After locking the door behind them, Michelle headed to the back of her house. "I'm going to change. I'll be right back."

"I brought a change of clothes, too."

"Use the hallway bathroom, and I'll meet you in the living room," Michelle said.

Tessa quickly changed into old jeans and a t-shirt before she stuffed her work clothes into the bag, and then washed her face and hands.

When she got to the living room, Michelle set glasses and plates down on the low sofa table. Not five minutes later, there was a knock on the door.

Michelle looked out the window before opening it. Nicole rushed in with several bags.

Tessa grinned. "What in the world did you get?"

Nicole chuckled and set everything down on the table. "Besides a couple of bottles of wine and the Chinese, I stopped by Betty's Bakery and got some brownies. We can't have a girls' night without chocolate."

Tessa groaned. She hadn't had them in a long time and was now salivating. The gooey fudge brownies were so good she could have eaten them every day.

The three sat around and consumed one bottle of wine with dinner. After they had eaten, they lounged around and drank a second bottle of wine while picking at their brownies.

"Talk to us," Michelle said.

Tessa thought she should probably stop drinking because her buzz was quickly becoming intoxication. But she couldn't. She felt more relaxed than she had in a while. Most of it had to do with the wine, but being with her friends was always fun.

She explained that Dominik had come up behind them when Dr. Farley was trying to flirt with her.

Nicole laughed. "Oh, God, I wish I could have seen his face when he saw Dominik."

Tessa grinned. "It was hilarious. What was also funny was the way he stayed as far away from me as he could today and didn't talk to me unless it was necessary."

"Good, that bastard has made it hard for several of us. Maybe Dominik scared him enough to stay away from all the women."

Tessa nodded. "I think he did."

Tessa went on to talk about the woman in the elevator and the ride home, how the night went slowly downhill, and how she went to bed alone for the first time she and Dominik had been together.

"What do you think is bothering him so much?" Michelle asked.

"I'm not positive, but he acted like he had thought about children but didn't want them with me."

The feeling of despair was still fresh.

"I can't believe that," Nicole said. "That man loves you more than anyone I've ever seen."

"I think he loves me, but I'm not positive. He said

a few things the first night we were together but nothing about feelings or the future since," Tessa told them.

"Guys are such pussies," Michelle growled.

Tessa and Nicole burst out laughing. The three didn't drink very often and were all feeling buzzed and loose.

Nicole raised her glass. "I agree with that."

Tessa just snorted and took another drink. "What should I do?"

"Could you just ask him what the problem is?" Nicole asked.

Tessa thought about it for a minute. "I don't know. I'm afraid of the answer. What if he's with me until Pierce is caught?"

"He asked you to move in with him," Michelle said.

"Yes, but the way he phrased it was because his house had better security and a bigger bed. Nothing has been said about making it permanent."

The three sat in silence for a minute.

"God, I don't know what I'd do," Nicole confessed.

Michelle patted her arm. "I say give it time. You guys have only been together for a little over four months."

Tessa nodded. "I'm planning on it, but I hate the awkwardness between us, and I don't know how to change it."

"Act normal," Nicole said. "Try to put it out of your mind for now. Put all your feelings out there. You don't have to say anything. I think the actions will speak for themselves."

Michelle nodded. "I agree."

"I'm horrible at pretending or lying," she said.

"Don't think of it like that," Michelle said. "Think

of it as keeping the peace for now."

Tessa thought about it for a moment and nodded. "Yeah. I'll try that. I'm glad we got together tonight."

"I am, too. We need to do this at least once a month," Nicole said.

Tessa smiled. "I'd like that. How about my place in a few weeks?"

"Sounds good," Michelle said and poured the last of the wine into everyone's glass.

Tessa had just finished her brownie and wine when someone knocked on the door. All three women stiffened until Tessa remembered Dominik was coming to pick her up.

"It's okay. It's Dominik. I didn't realize it was already nine," Tessa said and stood. She gasped as the room spun, and she bent to grab onto the sofa. "Whoa, I'm wasted," she said and then giggled.

The other two giggled and slowly tried to stand. Michelle finally got over to the door.

"Who's there?" she asked.

"It's me, Dominik."

Michelle unlocked and opened the door.

Tessa saw him step into the house, and the room suddenly felt very small. She was still trying to get her balance as she picked up her bag and giggled again when she swayed.

Dominik was by her side within a second, holding onto her. "How much did you have to drink, girls?"

"Just two bottles," Nicole said and then laughed.

Tessa saw Dominik frown.

"Nicole, how are you getting home?" he asked.

"I'm crashing here," Nicole said.

"We can take you home, too."

She shook her head. "No, but thank you. Michelle has a spare room."

"All right. I'll get Tessa out of here so you guys can go to sleep. If you need anything, call us," he said.

Tessa had her arms around his waist. He tightened his grip on her and used his other hand to carry her bag.

"Good night, guys," Tessa said.

"Night," the other two called out.

Dominik got her into the truck and put her seat belt on. By the time he climbed in, she was out.

Chapter Thirteen

Dominik stopped at the light and looked over at her. She looked so sweet lying there, and she even had a smile on her face.

He felt better having her with him. He'd been pacing at home for over an hour, giving her the time she wanted with her friends. If this happened on a regular basis, he thought he might eventually get used to it, but right then, it was torture not knowing if she was safe.

When they got home, he carried her into the house and then to the bedroom, sitting her down on the bed. He started to undress her.

She blinked and focused on him. "What are you doing?"

"I'm getting you undressed so you can sleep," he told her.

"I need a bath. I feel grungy from work."

He nodded and finished undressing her. "I'll start the water. I'll be right back."

When he came back, she was still awake but drowsy. He picked her up and carried her into the bathroom. He sat her in the bathtub. The water was halfway, and the bubbles he'd put in were overflowing.

Fortunately, she still had her hair up in a bun. He knelt beside her and began washing her, starting at her neck and moving down. He reached out to turn off the water when it got to her shoulders. He was glad he was close and had a hand on her because she started to fall asleep a few times.

He finished quickly, reached for the drain, and then lifted her out of the tub. He wrapped a towel around her and held her against his chest.

"Can you brush your teeth, Angel?"

She nodded.

He set her on her feet but kept an arm around her waist.

"Do you have to use the toilet?" he asked.

She shook her head.

"Okay, then let's get you into bed." He lifted her again and closed his eyes when she wrapped her arms around his neck and tucked her face against his chest. He could have stood there and held her like that all night.

He could tell she was falling asleep again, so he tucked her into bed. "I'll be right back."

He walked through the house to make sure everything was locked up and then turned on the security system before heading back to her. He checked on her before walking into the bathroom.

He tore off his clothing and showered quickly. He didn't want to go another minute without her in his arms.

After brushing his teeth, he turned off the lights and slid into bed beside her. He turned her and tucked her close against his body. He breathed in her feminine scent and exhaled. He couldn't see himself in bed without her for the rest of his life. She gave him a peace he hadn't known existed.

Dominik hadn't realized he'd fallen asleep until the sun shone in through the windows and woke him.

He glanced down to see Tessa still sleeping soundly. He carefully slipped from bed, dressed, and walked out into the kitchen. He started the coffee and then reached into the refrigerator for the carton of eggs.

It never failed to amaze him how much his house and life had changed since she came to live with him. It seemed every room, except his office, was organized and he hadn't realized how much time he took trying to find things before. He'd thought about asking her to organize his office with him but hadn't had a chance.

He planned on taking time today to sit Tessa down and talk. He hated the rift they had between them, and he wanted to mend it as soon as possible.

Dominik was stirring the eggs in the pan when Tessa's arms came around his waist. He immediately shut off the burner, turned to her, and wrapped his arms around her.

"How are you feeling, Angel?" he murmured against the top of her head.

"A bit nauseous and I have a slight headache, but otherwise pretty good."

"Why did you girls drink so much?" he asked.

She stiffened for a second. "We were just talking about girl stuff, and we hadn't spent a lot of time together lately."

He leaned back to look in her face and saw that she still had a wall up between them. He was more determined than ever to talk with her.

"Do you think you could eat some eggs?"

She shook her head. "Maybe a slice of toast and juice."

"I'll get it. Go and sit down."

He got her some juice and a few aspirin first before working on her toast. He didn't spread anything on it, not knowing if her stomach would handle it, but set the butter and jam on the table in front of her. He pressed his lips against the top of her head. "Eat, Angel."

She looked up and smiled. "Thank you."

"You're welcome."

Dominik sat down with his plate and coffee and started to eat. He watched her carefully but saw the color coming back into her face.

"What do you want to do today?" he asked.

She smiled. "Not much."

He chuckled.

"No, I thought about going to my house and cleaning. I haven't dusted or vacuumed since I moved in here with you."

He hated to think she still didn't consider his place her home and hadn't said anything about selling or even renting it out. Dominik decided to put it off since there was already a chasm between them that he wanted to take care of.

"How about I mow and weed-whack the lawn while you're inside? Maybe think about packing more of your things to bring here."

"I have everything I need here already."

He grew frustrated when she wouldn't look up at him. He sat his fork down. "Are you sick of living with me, Angel? I know I'm probably not great to live with. I've never lived with anyone except my mother, but I want to make you happy, so just tell me what you need from me."

She looked up at him in surprise. She sprang from her chair, walked to him, and then straddled his lap, facing him. "No, that's not it at all. I just don't want to rush anything." She hugged him tightly and pressed her face onto his neck. "Please don't ever think I'm unhappy with you because I'm not. I enjoy being with you so much."

His hands ran up and down her back. "Good. I'm not content unless I'm with you."

Dominik pushed her back a bit and then cupped her cheek. He took a moment to study her before dropping his head and kissing her. The moment their lips touched, heat raced through him and his cock immediately got hard. She made a desperate sound and tightened her grip on him.

He needed to be inside of her as deep as he could go. Only then would he feel whole.

Chapter Fourteen

Tessa let him take control. He stood with her legs wrapped around him and kissed him with all the emotion she felt.

When they got to the bedroom, he laid her on the mattress and stripped the clothing off her. She went up on her elbows when he started to undress.

"You make me feel very good when you look at me like that," he told her before coming over and pressing her back.

He cradled her face in his hands and started kissing her again. It didn't take long before she started to beg him to fuck her, but he just slowed down, making her grit her teeth.

Her eyes slid closed as he worked his way down her body, licking and nipping every part he could reach. He nudged her legs apart and moved in between them. Her eyes shot open and her back arched off the bed when he shoved his tongue into her cunt. That's all it took to push her over the edge. It felt like she was floating for a bit and then became aware he was still eating at her.

"Please, Dominik," she begged.

"I just need a little bit more."

Her thighs clenched in an agony of need, making her grip the blanket on either side of her hips and bite her lip to keep from crying out. She knew if she pushed him too much, he'd just take more time. Finally, he made his way up her body and in one strong lunge, pushed into her tight cunt.

Her nails dug into his shoulders as he started to ride her. There were no slow thrusts, he went straight for a hard, driving fuck. A scream tore from her lips as he threw her over the edge, and nothing mattered but the feeling of pleasure he built in her.

When she was coming down, she felt his cum spurt deep into her, throwing her over a third time.

Tessa lay there silently and concentrated on gaining some control. The strength of the fulfillment he gave her always stunned her, and it only seemed to get better every time. It made her wonder if it got stronger, whether she could have a heart attack, because it always felt like her heart would rip from her chest at any moment. The funny thing was, it wasn't painful, but it tended to overwhelm her at times.

He rolled them to the side and tucked her tightly against his body. They dozed for several minutes before he moved. He balanced himself on one elbow and looked down at her. He used his thumb to sweep the hair from her face.

"Do you want to go, Angel?"

She nodded and reached out to trace the scar on the side of his face. "I hate that you got hurt."

He grabbed onto her hand and kissed her palm. "I survived and got stronger."

She smiled. "Yes. And I'm so glad you did."

He bent and gave her a quick kiss. "If we don't get out of bed, we'll be spending the day here."

As much as she wanted to, they had things to do. "Let me shower and wash my hair."

He released her enough to let her slide from the bed.

Tessa grabbed some clothing and walked into the bathroom. It didn't take her long and she was headed into the kitchen. She was surprised he'd already cleaned everything and was out in the backyard. She walked to the open sliding door and looked out to find him wrapping up the hose. She could tell he'd watered the tubs of flowers she'd planted a few weeks after moving in.

"Are you ready?" he asked as he walked toward her.

Damn, he looked so hot in faded jeans and a black t-shirt. "Yes. I didn't take the time to dry my hair."

Dominik slid his fingers through the strands. "That's okay. It's warm enough out."

She followed him through the house, grabbing her purse from the table by the door. They had just gotten to the truck when his phone rang.

"Hello," he said as he reached for her door.

She could tell that whatever he was hearing pissed him off.

He stuck the phone in his pocket and sighed. "I have to go to one of the sites for a bit."

"That's okay. You can just drop me off at my house."

His face darkened. "I'd prefer you stay here."

"I can't go with you?"

He shook his head. "No, Angel. The place is dangerous, so you'd have to stay in the truck. At least here you can relax. Plus, you know this house is more secure than yours."

She looked down. God, she was so damn tired of feeling like a prisoner. She knew it wasn't his fault, though. She nodded.

"I promise to go as fast as I can. I'll be back before you know it," he told her.

"All right."

He led her back into the house. "Set the alarm after I leave. And stay in the house."

"I will." She tried to keep the sadness from her tone, but he caught it and came to her, wrapping his arms around her.

"I'm sorry, Angel. Pierce will eventually be

caught, and then we can relax a bit."

She rested her head against this chest. "I know. This is not your fault."

"Maybe not, but I'm as discouraged as you are. I don't want you to feel chained."

She didn't know how to take that, so she kept quiet. "You better get going."

He took her hand and pulled her back into the house. "Don't forget to turn on the security."

"I won't."

He kissed her quickly and shut and locked the door. "I want to hear it, Angel."

She rolled her eyes and pushed the buttons he'd shown her. "It's done."

"Good girl. I'll be back soon."

Tessa rested her forehead against the cool wood and listened as his truck drove away. The silence felt almost suffocating. She knew if she didn't keep busy, she'd go crazy. She walked into the kitchen and looked in the pantry. She was suddenly craving chocolate cake, so she decided to make one from scratch.

A few hours later, she was sitting at the kitchen table digging into a piece of cake when she heard Dominik pull in. She walked to the door, peeked out, turned off the security, and unlocked it.

His eyes ran swiftly over her as he walked to her. "Did you check before you opened the door?"

She nodded. "Yes. How did it go at the site?"

He moved inside and shut and locked the door. "Good. I got it figured out. They had picked up the wrong load of lumber. The load they had was for another job, so we had to go to one of the warehouses and get the right one."

She hadn't realized he had a warehouse, much less more than one. She wanted to know but would never ask how much he was worth. It made her uncomfortable to think he was a millionaire. God, if he found out how poor she really was, would he look at her differently? She only had a few more years to pay off her student loans, and then she'd be free.

"Do I smell chocolate?" he asked.

She laughed. "Yes. I made chocolate cake."

He looked surprised. "I didn't know you baked."

"I love to but rarely have the chance. Besides, I don't like making something because I hate to waste anything. I usually take stuff to the pediatric nurse's lounge."

"Now, you have me to feed."

She rolled her eyes at the grin on his face. "Come on, and I'll cut you a piece."

They sat at the table, talking and eating dessert. When she looked at the clock, it was too late to go to her house.

"I should find something to make for dinner."

He pulled her onto his lap when she passed. "No, let's order pizza and watch movies. What do you think?"

"I love the idea. I can't remember the last time I had pizza."

A little over an hour later, she leaned back against him with her head on his lap and groaned. "God, I ate too much," she complained.

He chuckled, rested his hand on her stomach, and started making slow circles.

Her eyes slid closed. "That feels good."

He kept at it as they watched the second movie of the night.

She couldn't get over how relaxed she felt with him. It was like they'd known each other for years instead of months. She tried to push away the doubts she still had and let herself enjoy him as long as she had him.

LILA FOX

Chapter Fifteen

Tessa rubbed her temple. She'd had a headache for a few hours and knew she should take some aspirin, but the day had been crazy, and she hadn't had a chance yet.

The phone rang at the nurse's station. "Hello."

"I need one of you nurses to come down to the ER and get a child that needs to be on your floor. She's been sitting in the room for over an hour, and we need the bed. It's been crazy today. Must be a full moon."

Tessa looked around and couldn't see anyone. "I understand. It's been like that here, too. I'll be right down." She called down to the main desk. "Is there a security guard available?"

"Not right now. They are having an issue in the ER. All the orderlies are busy, too. I can send one up as soon as they're free."

She couldn't wait that long. If all the security was needed, something bad had to be going on, and she wanted to get the child out of there. "No, that's fine. Thank you."

Tessa hung up and headed for the elevator. She knew she'd be fine if she used the elevator because there was always someone on them. She made it to the level the ER was on and headed that way. A hand came out of one of the closets, and before she could understand what was happening, he pulled her into it.

Her first look at the man made her blood run cold. Pierce. How the hell had he gotten into the hospital? When she recognized the orderly uniform he was wearing, it made sense.

The man hit the side of her head, making her head spin. She saw the duct tape he pulled out of his pocket and tried to fight.

"You fucking cunt. You've made my life a living hell, and you'll pay for it."

"They'll catch you, and then you'll be arrested," she cried out.

He tore off some tape and tied her hands together, the next one went over her mouth. The whole time, she struggled and pleaded. When the tape went on, it dug into her skin and made it hard to breathe.

She kept fighting him, but he would hit her wherever he could reach. When he started to pull her to the floor, her efforts doubled, and she started kicking. Things on the shelves started to fall to the floor. He had her pants over her hips, and then the closet door opened suddenly.

"Oh, my God! We need security. A nurse is getting attacked!"

Several people came into the room and dragged Pierce off of her. She was still fighting and trying to scream until a woman knelt beside her.

"Hey, you're from Pediatrics," she said. "I'm here to help you. It's okay now. The guy is down. I'm going to take the tape off, okay?"

Tessa nodded. She felt like she was being smothered because of the snot from her crying, clogging her nostrils. She took in a huge breath when the nurse pulled it off. She lay still on the floor, trying to calm her heart rate as the woman cut off the tape from her hands.

"We've got a stretcher here for you. We're going to take you to the ER."

Tessa shook her head and then grimaced.

"You have blood on your temple, and your lip is split. There might be more wrong we can't see."

Tessa reluctantly nodded. "Can you call Peds and tell them what happened? I've got several patients today."

"Yes. Let's get you on the gurney first."

Tessa was helped by two nurses and taken to the gurney. She heard a ruckus and looked down the hall to see Pierce being dragged down the hallway and several cops with the security guys.

"When you talk to the nurses on my floor have one of them call my guy."

"Sure. Let's get you in a cubicle first," the nurse said. "It's finally dying down, so you'll be able to see the doctor quickly."

"What about the child I was supposed to take up?" Tessa asked.

"Another nurse from the ER is taking her up now."

Tessa sighed and relaxed. She'd done everything she could for the moment and just wanted to rest.

She must have fallen asleep because when she opened her eyes, Michelle was standing by her side, tears running down her cheeks.

"Oh, God. I about had a heart attack when they told me what happened."

"Who's up on our floor?"

"Don't worry about that. Nicole is calling in a few nurses early. I called Dominik, and he's on his way."

Tessa nodded. The bright light made her head feel like it was splitting apart. Someone put a warm blanket over her.

"Hello, I see you're a nurse here. I'm new, so we haven't met yet. I'm Doctor Tremont."

"Hi," Tessa said.

"You're in shock, which is normal. The nurse is starting an IV. Let's take a look at your head."

Tessa held still and then flinched when he touched the spot that Pierce had hit repeatedly. She was vaguely aware of the needle going into the back of her hand, but the pain in her head overshadowed it.

"Do you feel nauseous?" the doctor asked.

"No."

"Let's check your pupils."

Tessa bit down on her lip when the pain soared through her. She grimaced again when she realized her lip was hurt.

"I don't think you have a concussion, and if you do, it's a mild one, but I'd like to take a CAT scan just to make sure."

Tessa didn't want one and didn't think she needed one, but she was too tired to argue.

Michelle patted her arm. "I'll wait here for Dominik."

"Thank you," Tessa said as they wheeled her away.

Thirty minutes later, they were wheeling her back. Her first look at Dominik made her stomach tighten. It looked like he was about ready to lose it. He visibly relaxed when he saw her and took her hand when they got her in place.

"Jesus, Angel. How do you feel?"

"I'm going to be just fine. My head hurts a bit, but they'll give me pain meds as soon as the doctor sees the scan."

His eyes traveled over her face, and he was careful when he touched her cheek.

She knew she probably looked like a mess.

"I received your scan," the doctor said. "It looks fine, so I can give you something for the pain. I also won't keep you overnight if you have someone with you."

"I'll be there with her every minute," Dominik said without looking at the other man.

"Good." The doctor said something to the nurse.

Tessa relaxed when she felt the medicine the nurse had given her start to mask the pain in her body.

"Is she hurt anywhere else?" Dominik asked.

"Mostly her head and arms, but you'll find a few bruises on her legs. Her whole body will be sore tomorrow," the doctor said. "I'll send home a few pain pills if she needs them. She can also use Tylenol for the pain."

Dominik nodded but still didn't take his eyes off her.

The doctor handed the nurse a chart. "She'll be ready to leave once the IV bag has emptied. I don't want her to go to work for at least three days."

She opened her mouth to argue but saw the determined look on Dominik's face and stayed silent.

Michelle came closer and gripped her arm. "I'm going to head back up to our floor. Please call if there is anything I can do."

Tessa smiled. "Thank you."

"You're welcome."

The cubicle was silent as the nurse walked out but said she'd be back to check on the IV.

"I really need you to hold me," she said.

He carefully picked her up and stepped over to the only chair in the room. She arranged her across his lap, making sure the IV wasn't pulling. She tucked her face against his throat, relaxed, and fell asleep. The adrenaline and pain medicine they gave her made it impossible to stay awake. She heard voices and felt the tape being taken off her hand and then the needle sliding out.

"Take the blanket, and I'll grab the bag her friend brought down and follow you out," the nurse said.

She felt him tuck her into the seat of his truck and put the seat belt on her. The rhythmic sound of the tires on the pavement put her deeper asleep. The next thing she knew, she was on their bed, and he was carefully taking her clothes off.

Tessa watched as he cataloged every scratch and bruise she received.

"Can I have a shower?"

He stared at her and then nodded. "I'll be in there with you. You're not strong enough to do it yourself."

"That's fine." She was glad he would help her because she was still so drowsy and knew she wouldn't be able to stand on her own for long.

Tessa thanked God for giving Dominik to her. She couldn't see her life without him.

Chapter Sixteen

Dominik washed and conditioned her hair before going over her body. When he was done, he wrapped a towel around her torso and sat her on the toilet seat.

"Are you okay for a second?"

She gripped the top of the towel and nodded.

He dried himself off and pulled on some boxers before grabbing another towel and squeezing as much water out of it as he could.

"Do you have enough energy for me to dry your hair a bit?"

"Yes. I'm still groggy from the pain medicine, but it's not horrible."

He'd worked on her hair for five minutes before her eyelids closed. He turned off the dryer. "That's good enough. Let's get you into bed."

He tucked her under the covers. "I'll be right back. I'm going to make sure everything is locked up and get you a glass of water and pills if you need them later."

She murmured something and turned on her side.

When he came back, he set everything on the nightstand and slid in behind her. He carefully arranged her against his chest.

Dominik pressed his lips against the back of her head, closed his eyes, and let his tears go. He couldn't remember being so scared since the first time she got attacked. He had so many questions he wanted answered, like why she was alone and how that bastard was able to impersonate an orderly. He knew he'd have to wait for them, but it just made his frustration more pronounced and harder to hide. He was glad she was asleep and didn't have to see his tears and fury.

She dozed off and on. He was able to get some

toast in her and coerced her to take one of the stronger pills.

He was jerked from sleep hours later when she cried out and started to move as if fighting.

"Angel, shhh. It's me, Dominik. Baby, wake up. You're safe at home with me." He kept talking until she finally awoke. She took one look at him, turned her face into his chest, and sobbed.

She had a few more bouts that night, and when the sun came up, they were both wrung out.

The next day, he made her lie on the sofa. It looked like she felt better and hadn't cried since early morning. He poured some juice and soup down her, which made her feel better.

It was late the following day when he felt she was strong enough to answer all his questions.

He held her on his lap with her head tipped back so he could see her expression. Tessa didn't know how the man got in, but she knew the hospital would investigate it. He wasn't happy about her leaving her floor alone but understood her reasoning. She had done everything right or to the best of her ability, so he couldn't fault her. It didn't help with the residual fear in him but he knew with time he'd get over it.

One good thing was Pierce would spend the next twenty years in prison, and Tessa hadn't been asked to go to court. The man had made a deal very quickly, knowing he could go away for a lot longer.

On the fourth day, she started complaining about wanting to go to work. Most of the damage done to her was gone, and she hadn't had a headache for several hours. It was the fact that he wouldn't be able to be with her that was driving him crazy. She had been attacked two times, and he hadn't been able to prevent it.

"Dominik, I swear, I feel better."

He sighed and pinched the bridge of his nose. He knew he couldn't keep her home any longer without it turning into a fight. "All right, but I want to take and pick you up."

"But Pierce is in jail," she said.

"I know, but it would make me feel better."

He could tell she was a bit discouraged but nodded, giving him his way.

Things slowly got back to normal, and he was happy he could still protect her to and from the hospital, but he saw something in her eyes as the days came and went, and it was scaring the shit out of him.

The thought of her wanting to leave him kept popping into his head, and he got nauseous every time.

He tried everything he could think of, but it didn't seem to help. He was at a loss on how to discuss it with her, so he had to wait for the other shoe to drop.

LILA FOX

Chapter Seventeen

Tessa stood looking out the back door of Dominik's house. She was no longer in danger since Pierce had been put away. Now, she had to deal with the situation with Dominik.

Since the day she'd been attacked at the hospital, Dominik had gotten quieter and quieter. She'd tried to talk to him a few times, but he had just changed the subject.

The only thing she could think of was that he wanted her to be gone but was afraid to say anything to her. She knew she'd have to take the first step, but she was terrified of losing him.

She sighed, opened the door, and walked out into the backyard. She sat in one of the loungers and hugged her legs to her chest. She prayed for the strength to do the right thing, but it was so hard. She'd never wanted anything the way she wanted him, and she knew the pain of losing him would cut deeper than anything else.

"Hey," he said behind her, making her jump.

She hadn't known he was home. She cleared her throat and put on a smile before she turned to him. "Hi, how was work?"

He studied her before walking toward her. "What's going on, Angel?"

She bit the inside of her cheek to keep from crying. "Not much."

Dominik slipped his hands into his pocket. "You look sad."

"I ... it's just that I have to decide what to do with my house."

She saw the curious and concerned expression fade on Dominik's face. "What about it?"

Tessa felt her nails dig into the palms of her hands. "I-I thought it was time I moved back."

She hated the hard look in his eyes. "You know I came here so you could protect me, and now that Pierce is in jail, there's no reason to stay, is there?"

Her stomach tightened. Oh, please, please, please ask me to stay. The seconds ticked by, and he just stood there. She had to clench her jaw to prevent her cry of pain.

Tessa moved off the lounge and started walking toward the house. "Well, okay. I guess I'll start to pack my things."

She didn't hear anything behind her and couldn't prevent the whimper of agony from escaping her mouth. She needed to get to the bathroom because she couldn't hold her tears in anymore.

The door closed behind her, and she slid down to the floor after grabbing a towel. She pressed her face into it and sobbed. She drew her knees up because the pain in her gut was more than she could take.

She had no idea how long she cried, but this bout of misery drained her, leaving her numb. She pulled herself to her feet and cringed at the first glance of her face. There was no way she'd be able to hide this from him. But then, he might not care enough to say goodbye.

After washing her face and blowing her nose, Tessa started to gather her things and pile them on the counter. When she thought she had everything, she opened the door and stopped short when she saw Dominik sitting on the side of the bed with his head bowed and his hands clenched together.

"Oh, I'm sorry. I'll go faster to get out of your hair."

His head snapped up. "Don't you dare put this on me."

Her brows pinched together. "What are you talking about?"

"I'm not the one asking to leave, you are."

"Are you saying you want me to stay?" She was afraid to hope.

"I certainly didn't ask you to leave," he snapped.

Her shoulders drooped. She didn't know what he wanted from her. "But you didn't ask me to stay either." She turned and walked into the closet and carried out one of her suitcases, setting it on the bed next to him.

"How can you not know I want you to stay?" he asked.

She looked at him. "When I came here, you talked about it being for my protection and the bed being bigger. In the months I've been here, you haven't said anything about what would happen after Pierce was caught. You never talked about a future together or how you felt about me."

"Why didn't you just ask me?" he asked.

"Because you've done so much for me already that I didn't want to put you on the spot or make you feel guilty." She angrily wiped a tear that escaped her cheek. He still didn't ask her to stay or have a future with her.

She turned abruptly and couldn't prevent the whimper she tried to hold back and went to the closet for some clothing. She came out and dumped the clothes into the suitcase.

"What do you want me to do?" he asked.

She hated to hear the anguish in his tone, but she couldn't comfort him when she was barely holding on.

She stood in front of him with her head bowed. "I don't want you to do anything you don't want to do. I'd never do that to you because I lo … care too much for you."

"Look at me, Angel."

She couldn't help but flinch at the nickname he'd given her, but she raised her head.

"I don't want us to end," he said.

"I don't either."

Silence filled the room.

"We can still see each other, Dominik. I can't see my life without you."

"Then why the fuck are you leaving?" he burst out.

"Because you haven't asked me to stay!" she yelled.

She wrapped her arms around her waist and waited. More silence. She couldn't take much more.

"So, I guess I'll keep packing," she said and turned from him.

"I want you to stay."

She looked over her shoulder at him. "I don't think I believe you. This is what I was afraid of."

"What?" he asked, confused.

"Of pushing you into doing something you don't want but think you have to."

"You're not making me do anything, Angel. I want you to stay."

"Then why haven't you said anything sooner? Why wait for me to pack to ask?"

"I didn't think I'd have to say anything. I thought you knew."

She threw her arms out. "How?"

"You know I love you…"

She shook her head. "No, I don't."

His brows snapped together. "I say it all the time."

She looked at him in shock. "Dominik, you've never told me you love me or that you want me to stay."

He looked confused. "Bull, I know I have said it."

She shook her head again. "Think about it."

She watched as he thought about what she was saying. She knew the instant he realized she was right.

"Fuck, Angel, I swear I feel like I say it twenty times a day."

"Maybe in your head, but I've never heard the words," she said.

He reached for her and pulled her into the spot between his widespread legs and then cupped her face in his hands. "Tessa, I love you more than I ever thought I could love someone. I fell in love with you the first time I saw you in the bar, and it's only grown deeper."

A tear slid down her face, and her hands gripped his wrists. "I love you, too. I knew that you were the other half of me the first time I saw you. I wanted so badly to crawl onto your lap and never get up."

He yanked her against his chest and held onto her tightly. They stood there in each other's arms for what felt like hours before he tipped his head back. "Angel, I love you, and I want you to live here for the rest of your life. I want you to sell your house because you'll never need it again. Is there anything else I need to say?"

She shed tears but smiled as she shook her head. "No. I love you too and never want to leave you."

"Hold on a second," he said, stood, and walked out of the room. He was back within a minute and sat back down. "I bought this the day after I first saw you, even though I didn't think we'd be together, and I fought it." He lifted the lid on the small velvet box and showed her a two-carrot, square-cut diamond. "Will you marry me?"

She stared at the ring in shock. It was the most beautiful thing she'd ever seen. "Yes. Yes, I will absolutely marry you."

She watched him smile for the first time all day,

take the ring out, and slide it on her finger.

"It fits perfectly," he said.

He was right. She felt almost dizzy going from one extreme emotion to the other, but she couldn't be happier. She hugged him tightly. "You are my world."

His hands slid up and down her back. "And you are mine."

Chapter Eighteen

She moved as if to step back, but he didn't want to release her.

"There's only one more thing I need to know."

He looked at her face. "What?"

"Children. I want children, but if you are against it, I can live without them."

He sighed. "I want them, too, but I'm terrified of what carrying a large baby will do to you. I was over ten pounds, and my mom always told me how much damage I did to her body and how I almost killed her."

Tessa gasped. "That's horrible. Why in the world would a mother tell her child that?"

"My mother is a selfish, shallow bitch, and she never cared about me," he said bluntly and without anger or resentment. He learned it was just the way she was, and he'd never be able to change her. He tried getting her clean a few times and even bought a condo for her in a better part of town. He made the mistake of putting it in her name, and within a few months, she'd sold it, took the money, and went back to where she started. He'd just given her the means to become more addicted, and she was now into drugs.

"She only cared about the money the State gave her for me. She never spent it on me, and that's why I started working so young."

"How about we wait and see what a doctor says?" she said. "If he feels it won't be good for me, I'd like to think about either fostering or adopting some children. There are so many of them out there that have little to no chance at a good life."

He nodded. "I really like that idea. I think we should check into it even if we can have a child."

He knew he'd said the right thing when Tessa smiled brightly.

"I want you to put your things away. I'm going to make a call, and then we'll go on a picnic to celebrate our engagement. Either later today or tomorrow, we should go to the other house and pack the things you want to bring over. If it's a lot, I can call in a few of my men."

She snorted. "Are you in a rush?"

"Yes. I'll feel better when this is the only home you have," he told her.

She ran her hands over his shoulders. "How about we celebrate our engagement here and now and then go on a picnic later?"

Dominik grinned at the mischievous smile on her face. "Oh, so how are we going to celebrate?" he asked, knowing the answer.

Tessa pushed him to his back and crawled up on top of him. "Like this," she said and proceeded to kiss him.

The passion exploded, and the need for each other increased. He rolled until she was under him without breaking the kiss. He tore off her clothing and then his own and then entered her with one long, deep thrust.

Both groaned at the delicious sensation of being whole that they could only get with each other. He braced his weight on his elbows as he started to surge into her, slowly building the savage ecstasy and heated desire.

She tightened on his cock, but he could tell she was fighting it. He understood because this time, it felt like their souls were meshing, and they would never be the same, but he wasn't going to allow her to hide from it.

He reached around her cupping her ass. "Let yourself go, Angel."

She still resisted.

His big, blunt finger slid between the cheeks of

her ass, and after swiping some of the copious syrup running from her, he thrust it into her ass as far as it would go. A strangled, wild cry burst from her, filling the room with the cries of ecstasy.

Brutal slashes of pleasure raced down his spine, and then there was relief when his cum spurted from his cock and filled her cervix. He lay there for a long time trying to gain some control before he slipped his finger from her ass, and then he slid his cock out of her cunt. He pressed a quick kiss on her lips.

"I'll be right back."

After washing, he walked back in with a wet cloth and cleaned the evidence of their passion from her.

He tossed the washcloth aside and crawled into bed, wrapping her in his arms. "How are you doing?"

She hummed and rubbed her cheek against his chest.

He grinned. He let them rest for an hour before he decided to get up. "Let's get dressed, Angel. I'll call Cecil's Diner and get food for our picnic ordered. How does that sound?"

She smiled at him. "I like it."

She started to move away from him, but he yanked her back, making her scream. He smiled at her. "I love you, Angel."

She sighed and cupped his cheek. "I love you, too."

A while later, they found an area by a creek in one of the parks. They spread the blanket out and then started pulling things from the basket.

"Oh, my, this looks great," she said.

Dominik nodded. "I heard one of the guys talking about it. I'll have to thank him."

The afternoon sun faded, but they didn't want the picnic to end. When a cool breeze made Tessa shiver, he knew he had to get her home.

They packed everything up and walked to the truck. He got her situated in her seat with her belt on before he started to drive them home. He took her hand.

"Hey, what would you think about flying to Vegas and getting married? That's unless you want a wedding."

Her mouth dropped open, and then she clapped. "I love the idea. When can we go?"

"How about next weekend? Can you take off Friday?" he asked.

"I think I can get someone to work my shift," she said.

"Good. We'll fly out Thursday night and go shopping for a dress for you before we get married. Then we can spend a few days touring the city before we fly home on Sunday night."

"That would be so much fun. I won't tell my friends because they might get mad that we didn't invite them."

"In the next few weeks, we can host a dinner at one of the upscale restaurants in town with our closest friends."

Tessa nodded. "That would be great."

"I thought about going to your old house, but I think we're too wiped out. I'd rather go home and cuddle on the sofa and watch a movie. Is that okay with you?"

"Yes. That sounds wonderful. It's been an eventful day."

He lifted her hand and kissed her knuckles. "Yes, it has, but it's also been the best day of my life."

She looked at him with tears in her eyes but a smile on her face. "For me, too."

Epilogue

Dominik walked through the door to his house to hear what sounded like a party in his backyard. He walked to the slider door and saw his beautiful wife of five years and their three adopted children: one girl and two boys. There were also a few other kids he recognized as his children's friends, and they were all playing football.

After they got back from their wedding in Vegas, they went to see a gynecologist specialist to see if it would be dangerous for her to carry and give birth to a child. The doctor had done several tests, one of them being a special ultrasound, and found her pelvis was too small to carry a large baby. He had thought she would be upset, but when he asked her, she just smiled.

Tessa shook her head. "Not really. I think with our childhoods, we're the best people to adopt the kids no one wants."

Within a few weeks, they had a foster child, and if things worked out, they could adopt the boy. He had become a part of his family easily, and Dominik could tell Tommy, the first child, was so grateful to finally have a home and family of his own.

He'd been in the system for eleven years since he was a baby because of an issue with his spine. After seeing a specialist, the doctor decided the boy had grown out of whatever issue the foster system thought he had.

Tessa and he talked about the fact that everything could have been normal this whole time, but no one took the time to get him checked. The other two had fallen onto their laps and had easily become part of the family.

Dominik walked outside and over to his wife, who was grilling hamburgers. She jumped when he wrapped an arm around her waist.

"You scared me," she said and frowned at him over her shoulder.

"I'm sorry." He tried his best not to smile.

Tessa's eyes narrowed. "Really?"

He nodded. "Sure."

She snorted but turned in his arms and raised her face for a kiss.

Like every other time they touched, they couldn't get enough of each other. The hooting and hollering of the children got their attention. He chuckled when he saw the blush on Tessa's face.

"It's okay for them to see us kiss, Angel."

She tapped his arm. "Yes, but I could feel your hand inch down to my ass."

"It's a habit."

She rolled her eyes and handed him the spatula. "Here, grill the meat while I go in and make a salad."

He pressed a quick kiss to her forehead and turned to the grill.

"Oh, by the way…" she said.

He knew what was coming before she could say it.

"The counselor at the orphanage has a child she thinks needs us," Tessa said.

He looked at her and sighed. "I'm going to have to add onto the house, aren't I?" They had already taken all the bedrooms with their three kids, and they didn't want them to have to share.

She smiled sweetly. "Yes. That would be wonderful."

Before he could say anything, she turned and walked into the house, and one of the boys yelled at him.

"Dad, come and throw the ball with us."

Every time he heard them call him "Dad," his

heart melted. He knew there would be more, and he didn't mind adopting other kids. He and his wife were loving, had enough money, and understood them better than anyone, and they both had enough love for several more.

He'd have to make up additional plans and get his guys on it. He was thinking of three more bedrooms. Scratch that. He knew his wife well. He'd build six new rooms with three more bathrooms. Hell, he could always add on later if the family grew. He just hoped she'd stop at eight, but that probably wouldn't happen.

The End

LILA FOX

EVERNIGHT PUBLISHING ®

www.evernightpublishing.com